DARKSCAPES

# DARKSCAPES

*by*

*Anne-Sylvie Salzman*

Translated by William Charlton

Tartarus Press

*Darkscapes*
by Anne-Sylvie Salzman
translated by William Charlton
First published by Tartarus Press 2013 at
Coverley House, Carlton-in-Coverdale, Leyburn,
North Yorkshire, DL8 4AY, UK

This edition published 2020

The publishers would like to thank Jim Rockhill
for his help in the preparation of this volume.

# CONTENTS

I

LOST GIRLS

# CHILD OF EVIL STARS

EVERY year in October Gluck's Circus comes to Groddeneck and installs itself under the lime trees beside the river. Groddeneck is its last stop before the season in Vienna. The gypsies stay for a month; during the day they repaint their wagons and attend to the animals; in the evening they set up the big top. 'Gluck' is no more than a name. The last Gluck died of old age and his two children sold the enterprise to his manager, a former seaman called van Aalsen. He was a cold, polite man who liked nothing so much as dogs. He was never to be seen in the ring with the new Gluck; only the ostriches, the sea lions, the zebras, a black panther that always walked with a strut, the lions, and the elephant Mawarathi which its Indian mahout (whom some made out to be Hungarian) had trained to write its name with flowers—daisies—in the circus sawdust.

Van Aalsen had saved the circus from bankruptcy and from arson at the hands of unscrupulous mountebanks. The criminals had been handed over to the authorities, but at night, surrounded by his dogs (of which he had five, all sleeping under his caravan) he never failed to make the round of the encampment.

Friedrich on two successive evenings saw the former sailor passing beneath his windows, the big dogs trotting at his heels with lithe and silent tread. Friedrich lived in a villa built several years before on the edge of the fairground. Having come as a simple student from Vienna he had married a Groddeneck heiress, the daughter of the director of the Imperial and Royal

1

Hospital. When wife, children and servants had all retired to bed Friedrich often remained in the drawing room with the lights extinguished, and watched the alley which ran beside the fairground. Even when the circus was not there, there were passers-by. It was the shortest route from the station to the brasserie Bayern. From behind his curtains Friedrich spied idly upon the working girls. Often he recognised patients, or wives or mothers of patients, from Wing B of the Imperial and Royal Hospital, the wing of which he was doctor in charge and where they treated diseases of the lungs.

On the third of October Friedrich went out by himself to dine with his friend Johann Fuchs, and returned too late to see the passage of van Aalsen and his dogs. Frau Friedrich never accompanied her husband to Fuchs's: his flat was too ill maintained, she said, and smelt of frog. Fuchs, who nourished secret and hopeless feelings for his friend's wife, was glad of this quarantine. The smell, which was quite real, came from two large glass tanks he kept in his study. In them lived salamanders and toads which Fuchs sometimes used for purposes of experiment. He was a neurologist; some seven years junior to Friedrich, he had the complexion of a girl and large eyes of a deep and languorous blue. That evening Friedrich found him in his dressing gown, bent over a tiny black corpse he continued skilfully dissecting with a minute scalpel, while Friedrich took off his overcoat.

It was one of the salamanders, dead from no apparent cause.

'Old age?' suggested Friedrich, and Fuchs shook his head.

'I should say rather boredom, and indigestion from a surfeit of flies, since she no longer has to go hunting them.'

The woman in charge of the building went out to fetch a dish of lamb shank and turnips from a neighbour who cooked for the doctor on occasion, also a pudding with raisins and beer. The two friends ate in the sitting room, which was not so musty as the study. Friedrich smoked a cigar and Fuchs drew his friend in profile on the margin of a programme from Gluck's Circus.

'I didn't know you were a fancier of girl circus riders,' said Friedrich.

'There aren't any girl riders at Gluck's, worse luck,' said Fuchs, and just behind Friedrich's ear appeared the smile of the beautiful Frau Friedrich.

'The maid has taken the children there,' said Friedrich.

'Happy maid—happy children.'

'How do you know that there are no girl riders?'

'I didn't see any in the parade,' said Fuchs with a serious air.

The following day they visited the fairground, the animals in their cages and the gallery of monstrosities. It was the monstrosities that Fuchs desired to see, the kitchen girl having specially praised the human serpent. Fuchs had very fixed ideas about the evil the mind sometimes inflicts on the body. Van Aalsen had set up his new attraction, the great Pavilion of the World Beyond Belief, beside the river. The visitors entered in restricted numbers through a small entrance-lobby draped in green silk where two turbaned men of coppery skin stood with crossed sabres before a door of carved wood which opened and shut always in silence. The sabres separated and you entered, in a spirit of cynicism or trepidation, down a long corridor which smelt, Fuchs murmured with some surprise, of the urine of wild beasts. On either side of this passage animals and monstrosities alternated in cages shut off by sheets of glass, high and thick. Friedrich and Fuchs first saw the lion, couched against a painted landscape—a setting sun, a castle of ancient Spain. Shadows passed before the glass. There were little cries: 'Mummy! The lion! The lion!'

In the next window a live dwarf was riding a stuffed calf, a monstrosity with two heads placed in a blue-green prairie, by the light of a painted moon. The dwarf was singing with closed eyes an unintelligible song. Friedrich had already disappeared into the darkness of the passage and Fuchs put his hand on the glass, intrigued. 'Poor fellow, seated all day long on a dead animal that recalls to him in one way or another his own deformity; all day he sees us bloated idiots going by, no better than he is.' The dwarf, however, had a sort of smile on his lips. A hand descended on the shoulder of the doctor.

'Oh, Doctor Fuchs!'

By the light of the tableau vivant Fuchs recognised one of his patients; two children were hiding under her skirt.

'Doctor, have you seen the wolves? My God, I don't know....'

Fuchs went to see the wolves. There was the sound of low laughter, a scuffle in the safety of the darkness.

In the wolf cage a girl of twelve or thirteen with hairy arms and legs, her lips twisted by a deep cleft, was sleeping between two hairless wolves. People pressed forward to look at her harelip.

'But it's ugly, all the same. What is horrific, they say, is to see her eating raw meat. . . . In Russia, it's said, and in times gone by. . . .'

But the man Fuchs had seized by the arm was not Friedrich. He gave the doctor a light shove, pushing him against the window, and moved away with an oath.

'Oh! My God!'

There was a crowd in front of the snake pit, and Fuchs, who was more bothered, curiously, by the smell of mammals than by that of reptiles, found himself at the base of the window, forehead and hands pressed against the glass.

'Isn't that the monster you wanted to see?'

The circus painters had erected two weedy palm trees at the mouth of a plaster cave. The tail of a boa-constrictor, living or dead, hung down one of the trunks. Fuchs instinctively searched with his eyes the inside of the cave. Slowly there impressed themselves on his retina, and then on his brain, the contours of a shape that was vaguely human: face, neck and trunk undulated with a single motion. Two dark slits appeared in the middle of the shape, and expanded. A gleaming gaze fixed itself upon Fuchs's eyelids, soft as a tongue. A child started to scream, and Fuchs, his stomach turned, went out at a run by the Indian vestibule.

The swords of the guards were of cardboard like everything else. Outside, a misty sun was shining through the branches of the fairground trees upon fresh faces. Fuchs went past an enclosure where two circus girls in men's trousers were practising their acrobatics. Strong thighs, round breasts, downy faces, the girls came, they told him, from Kiev; they were sisters. Their mother was the laundress for the circus. They spoke a rather shy German.

'Tell me, it's new, this . . .'—and Fuchs pointed to the World Beyond Belief, on the gable end of which a wooden owl was spreading wide its wings.

'Yes, Mr van Aalsen bought it in Holland,' replied one of the girls. 'We've had it only a year.'

'Have you seen the dwarf?' asked the other, 'the dwarf on the calf? It was from him, Pedersen, that Mr van Aalsen bought the whole thing.'

They looked at one another, fingers on lips, giggling.

CR

Friedrich was waiting for Fuchs near the river.

'So where have you been?'

After they separated Friedrich had followed in the wake of a short round lady accompanied by three children—the partridge and her chicks, he told himself. It seemed to him as if the wild beasts of the World Beyond Belief looked menacingly upon this bird-woman as she passed. He observed that in the light of the windows to the exhibits she resembled rather a caricatured octopus, with her bulging forehead, protruding eyes, beaky little nose, and almost invisible mouth. As for her children, he did not even try to make out their traits. One of them having placed its small hand on the glass, it became suddenly rosy and transparent; Friedrich's heart revived. In the crowd which was waiting for the battle between the cobra and the mongoose—it was one of the show-pieces of the tent; a young Indian seated on a card-board rock would urge on the little gladiators—Friedrich lost sight of the octopus and her children; the current swept him into a corner. A coppery hand grasped his elbow.

'Yes?'

'Doctor, at the dawn of time there were human forms which evolution rejected and consigned to oblivion. They were obliter-ated, surviving only in myths. For us they are reborn. Come.'

The voice was clear and firm. Friedrich fancied he could detect the smell of honeysuckle.

'Can it be that without knowing it I have a patient from the circus?'

Friedrich passed between two hangings which the steady hand parted. On the far side the air was fresher; the noise of the crowd was barely audible; there was solitude. Friedrich took a step towards the hidden cage. The décor portrayed a seaside beneath a pale sky. A woman was sitting on the shore—but was it a woman? Her long hair fell over thin shoulders. Her back was turned to Friedrich, who tapped lightly on the glass. The woman hunched her shoulders. Never had Friedrich seen skin so bloodless, even in the wing for pulmonary disorders. At last she stood up. She was clad in a tunic of Grecian cut, made of silk or white cotton. Her weak legs could hardly support her. Her downcast head and long, lustreless hair concealed her face. She took a few steps towards Friedrich.

'Who are you?'

He tapped again on the glass, his heart beating. She raised her head and in a face which some unknown affliction had entirely demolished and reconstructed, he saw a single eye blink. He must have made a movement of alarm. The prisoner fell on her knees before the window that separated them and spread both hands flat upon the glass at the level of her face.

CR

'Do you know that they have a cyclops-woman there?'

'I think,' replied Fuchs, 'that I no longer have any desire to know what they have there.'

'You haven't seen her?'

Friedrich heard his own voice trembling, and did not insist.

They walked in silence to the hospital where Fuchs, as he often did, passed part of the night. Friedrich was surprised to find himself envying his friend. In the quiet of the night the gaze of the cyclops-girl came back to him; and at the thought of it he saw in his mind's eye her awkward limbs and her hair falling to her waist. He continued thinking of her the following evening throughout a party to which he had invited doctors and their wives. Everywhere he saw the prisoner's eye gleaming. In the end he could not look at his daughters playing ball in the garden without seeing again the monstrosity on her knees. But the violence of his agitation at the vision caused it at last to disappear; he did not recall it even when he went to bed, but fell asleep at once.

On the two days that followed Friedrich managed to stop himself from going again to see the unfortunate girl. Had she a name, poor thing, or had her horrified parents cast her off without giving her anything? 'You, Friedrich: what would you have done with such a monster?'

He saw himself on a winter evening, the baby in his arms, walking to a frozen lake, making a hole in the ice, and letting the infant slide under it to be seized at once by the cold. This picture came to him when he was examining a young patient: it arose from the sight of the little girl's skinny back, so similar to that of the Child of Evil Stars. After the girl had been settled back in bed Friedrich went on to see Fuchs and when he could not find him either in his office or in the psychiatric wards, he set off, almost against his will, for the fairground.

A queue was already forming around the red and green entrance to the big top. Friedrich there perceived several children and the people in charge of them gesticulating and laughing loudly. The surroundings of the World Beyond Belief were no more tranquil. A dozen cavalrymen in uniform from the barracks in the town were bargaining over the entry price. 'Hey, but, sweetie, who's going to defend you if war breaks out?' One of them crushed a thick cigar stub under the heel of his boot. 'Hey, darling, is it true that inside you can see a dwarf riding a unicorn?'

Friedrich felt dizzy. His intestines grumbled. At the entry to the gallery his forces suddenly deserted him, even though he could feel springing up at the very bottom of his miserable intestines an irrepressible joy. They were all there: the dwarf on the calf, the human serpent, the human tree, the wolf girl, and Friedrich in the hope-filled darkness thought he had reached the end when one of the Indians took him gently by the arm.

'Sir, we are about to shut.'

'But I haven't . . .'

'I am very sorry, sir. When the circus opens, the gallery shuts. We are all needed in the ring.'

How could he reply to that? Friedrich followed the guard, though at the same time from the corner of his eye he could just see, in the depths of the World Beyond Belief, the bluish patch made by the light of the cage of the Child of Evil Stars, suddenly obscured by a curtain of hair.

In front of the entry to the circus there still stretched the queue of people waiting. The cavalrymen had joined it and were chaffing the barmaids. Friedrich went on his way. What vicious master was it that had made the Child of Evil Stars dance on the stage? So it was that he went home pensive, and kept his eyes upon the happy faces of his daughters and his wife. An uncle had brought the children a puppy, a terrier no bigger than two clenched fists. 'Daddy, have you seen it, daddy?' Friedrich duly went to see the puppy, for which the nanny had made up a little bed in the nursery. When the girls were settled for the night Friedrich went down again to the drawing room. His wife, sitting at the piano, was reading a score. She had let down her hair, and was nibbling the end of a red and blue pencil.

'Have you seen the dog?'

She had long, shining chestnut hair, her eyes were large and dreamy, her lips firm. Beneath her skin there quivered a vital directness unknown to Friedrich.

'Your brother didn't wish to stay for dinner?'

'He's gone back to Vienna,' said Frau Friedrich, her brows knitted. 'Tell me, how are things with your friend Fuchs? Frau D thought he looked thin. Why does he never come to see us any more?'

'You don't like him,' said Friedrich, putting his hand on his wife's hair.

'That's not true,' said Frau Friedrich half closing her big sleepy eyes. 'His flat is disgustingly dirty, I agree, but he himself, no.'

'Then I shall ask him to dine with us this Friday,' said Friedrich. 'You will see that he behaves charmingly, and that your Frau D is nothing but a chatterbox.'

Frau Friedrich smiled through the shining veil of her hair, and Friedrich, stabbed in the pit of his stomach by a pang of love, stood up with a cough and went to hide his emotion at the window.

Two or three nights passed which augmented the doctor's malaise. When evening came he no longer, as had been his custom, stayed at the window looking onto the fairground, in order to smoke a few cigarettes before going to join his wife. A desire mixed with bitterness had come back to him for the body, just the body, of his wife. But when he lay close to her and felt the contact of her skin all down his legs, there returned to him like a ridiculous punishment the vision of the ill-starred child with her halting step. 'It is close to her that I ought to be.' In any case Frau Friedrich did not respond to this rekindled flame. Once in bed this baffling woman always fell asleep. Two years after the birth of their second daughter she had ceased to encourage the amorous impulses of her husband. Friedrich had not taken offence, and went at least once a month to the brothel.

'That woman, that unfortunate . . .' Eyes wide open in the night Friedrich, suddenly exhausted, raised his hands towards the ceiling and spread his fingers. 'Poor monstrosity.'

During the night, which was cloudy, nothing could be seen of the circus except one or two intermittent lights. Van Aalsen and his dogs had gone to bed long before. 'Tomorrow I shall go and see Fuchs.' This reassuring thought kept him company till morning. At one time he saw his friend's face appear on the ceiling, his eyes bright and tender; at another he was in a conversation constantly renewed on the road which ran beside the river, a walk the two friends had often taken when they first met. But the memory of Fuchs lost force in the course of the night. In the end Friedrich saw him in the dark galleries of the World Beyond Belief, and from behind. He stood before the window of the Child of Evil Stars, his arms spread wide and his shoulders shaking under the influence of evil laughter. At last in a mood of deep bitterness Friedrich fell asleep.

He had this dream. His wife was stretched out on the grass in the shadow of a tree the flowers of which were being gradually blown away by the wind. On her stomach she held a creature that she tenderly called 'my baby' but in which Friedrich, horrified, could see only a sort of huge worm totally covered with fur, and equipped at one end with the rudiments of two eyes and a mouth.

This monster had not been exhibited at the World Beyond Belief.

The following day Friedrich went dispiritedly across the fairground. The circus people had lit a fire near the ticket office for the gallery and were making coffee. It was now late in October, and at the end of the month, Friedrich seemed to remember, the gypsies would depart. His heart began to thump. He shut his eyes and the white throat of a frog appeared on the black and green inside of his eyelids. He quickened his step to get away from the merriment he envied in the little troop.

Fuchs lived in a seedy block of flats on the square for the flower market, which had not been held for twenty years. An old woman was swilling down the pavement. Friedrich had hardly rung the bell before she set down her bucket and raised her hands towards the sky. 'Is it Dr Fuchs that you're coming to see? He left this morning for Goerres. He said his mother had just died.'

A long slender blade pierced Friedrich's side. 'My God! My God! My poor friend!' But was his sorrow genuine sympathy, or selfish chagrin because he could not confide to Fuchs his new obsession, in the course of a walk along the river outside the town?

The old woman let him in. Perhaps the doctor would like to speak to the woman in charge? Friedrich did not know about that. But he liked the ill cleaned flat of his friend and its dissection room, in which he remained for a while sitting and smoking a small disintegrating cigar that was left lying on Fuchs' desk. The woman referred to never showed up. Friedrich, his gaze absent, made a tour of the little tanks, examining the batrachians his friend was rearing. He remembered how as a child he had secretly kept in his room a salamander which he had found in the garden. It died of hunger when he was staying with his aunt in Salzburg; full of the joy of city life he had forgotten it. On his return he found the animal's little corpse in the box where it had lived. On its back there had grown up vertically a forest of spectral mould.

Before his hasty departure Fuchs had drawn on his writing paper several grotesque faces, among which Friedrich recognised a woman patient and the wolf girl. He took up the pencil, sharpened it with his penknife, and added a hat with flowers to the portrait of the patient. The lead of the pencil broke, and Friedrich mechanically slipped it into his pocket. It was time to get back to the road and the bright sky of a deceitful autumn. Fondling the pencil in his pocket Friedrich went with bent head through the town. In front of the hospital two men were fighting under the muzzle of a horse. About to cross the road, Friedrich saw one of them carry his hands to his eyes, which were gushing tears of blood. His yelps could still be heard from the porch.

Friedrich occupied a modest office on the first floor of the wing for pulmonary diseases, between the library and the examination room. It often happened, on days when he was on duty, that he fell asleep in one of the large armchairs in the library. There was no leisure for that this morning. Van Aalsen, without his dogs, was awaiting him in his office. He had his back to the window, his arms folded, and a sombre expression.

'Yes?'

'I am van Aalsen, from Gluck's Circus,' said the man.

'I know.' Friedrich felt a qualm of nausea. 'Please sit down, Mr van Aalsen.'

'I have come,' said the Dutchman, 'on behalf of one of my people. It is a difficult case. They tell me you are a lung specialist; is that right? Would you be able to come and see the person at our place? You see, she isn't able . . . she wouldn't be able to leave us.'

Van Aalsen gazed over Friedrich's shoulder, his eyes open wide.

'Sickness where for all the world there is nothing but gaiety and song—it is strange. Will you come to the circus, doctor?'

*It is the Child of Evil Stars: the ill-starred child is dying.*

'Certainly I will come, Mr van Aalsen. I'll come with you now, if you wish.'

'But have you not sick people to visit, and appointments? They told me at the reception that you were very busy, doctor.'

'Let's go now,' said Friedrich. Van Aalsen's hesitations and his gloomy liquid gaze were delaying the moment when he should meet up again with the Child of Evil Stars.

Two big circus dogs were couched on the seats of van Aalsen's gig. They raised their heads at their master's return, jumped down silently from their seats and trotted behind the gig on the way to the fairground. Van Aalsen led his two dogs without speaking, and Friedrich counted off the minutes with a terrible joy. The sun was shining low in the sky through clouds; two bright points appeared on either side of it. The gig passed in front of the World Beyond Belief and came to a stop beside the big top.

'It's at the end of the month that you leave for Vienna?'

'Yes,' said the circus master in a low solemn voice. 'We always spend the Christmas season in the capital. Every year the Archduke comes to see us.'

One of the Indians from the World Beyond Belief, clad in a bronze green tunic, was waiting for them near the big wagons.

Van Aalsen passed him the reins. The man looked at Friedrich and smiled.

'Doctor,' asked the Dutchman, 'are you familiar with our ways? Have you visited our . . . our galleries?'

Friedrich nodded. The nearness of happiness rendered him dumb. The Indian, with the gesture he had used before among the showcases, placed a hand on his arm and pushed him gently towards the door of the caravan.

The sick girl had been laid in the brass bed of van Aalsen, which his dogs had vacated. With her head enclosed in a bag of white silk she was sleeping a tormented sleep, arms and legs thrashing beneath the bedclothes with convulsions. Van Aalsen took a position at the bedside and the Indian, the circus infirmarian, Friedrich realised, placed his two hands under the foot of the bed, his eyes shining with tears. 'It is he,' thought Friedrich 'who has sent for me, and it is indeed the Child of Evil Stars.'

Van Aalsen looked away all the while that Friedrich, feeling devastated, was examining the patient. He found her deeply consumptive and feverish, at death's door. The Indian had raised her delicately to a sitting position, taking care that her white silk hood should not slide off. 'Why do you hide her from me?' Friedrich wanted to say. 'You know perfectly well that I have seen her in her naked misery.' At each breath taken by the child of misfortune, the material clung to the strange shape of her face. Under Friedrich's hand the weak muscles quivered, the skin contracted, bathed in an acid sweat. In a corner of the little room van Aalsen lit an incense-burning brazier.

'It is a case of tuberculosis, and I am afraid very advanced,' said Friedrich at last, while the Indian tenderly settled the sick girl back in the bed. 'What happened that made you call me?'

'Yesterday evening she started to vomit blood.'

'But before that?'

Van Aalsen shook his head. Friedrich saw the prisoner, her two hands on the glass of her cage, and then the film of blood on the glass.

'Doctor, one could never know what she was thinking. She was dumb, on top of all her other misfortunes. What must be done, doctor—Doctor Friedrich?

'She must go to hospital, of course,' said Friedrich. 'This young woman is very seriously ill; her condition requires constant attention, if she is to be saved.'

'Go to hospital?'

Van Aalsen slowly nodded, and the Indian lowered his eyes.

'I understand your fears,' said Friedrich. 'I shall take care that she is protected from having people stare at her. But your quarters, with the animals and the damp from the river. . . .'

'Oh, yes, yes. . . .'

She shivered incessantly under the blanket, but without a murmur. Friedrich, after a last futile examination, stood up, his head swimming from the reek of her skin.

'Tomorrow morning, gentlemen, I shall send one of our ambulances.'

'Do you think, doctor, that she could go with us to Vienna?

'I very much doubt it,' replied Friedrich. 'And if she could, it must be understood that there could be no question of exhibiting her.'

'Naturally, naturally,' babbled van Aalsen, he eyes starting from his head under the influence of a sudden terror. What was he seeing? What hideous monster-hunt was he remembering? The Indian accompanied Friedrich as far as the exit from the fairground. Night was falling. A sound of happy voices floated from the big top, interrupted by pants of ecstasy. In Friedrich's house all the lights were out, and he remembered that his wife and daughters were at the opera, where a work was being performed he did not like. He entered by the door onto the garden, passed through the kitchen, and mounted to his study

15

without meeting anyone. 'Still, the servants. . . . What's become of them?' The maids, probably, were in their room, and Hermann, the manservant, was asleep in the library, awaiting the return of his master and mistress. 'Or perhaps he's with the women.' As he climbed the stairs he was conscious at each step of the weight and weariness of his body. The muscles of his thighs were stiff. Several times he had to stop and catch his breath before he reached his study. The oil-lamp he carried weighed more than his heavy instrument case; its wavering light threw shapeless shadows on the corners of the stairs. Arrived at last in his study Friedrich thought he saw a little whitish animal, a lamb, perhaps, with big shining eyes that reminded him of Fuchs, running out of the room and keeping by the wall.

'Idiot that I am. It's our terrier, the puppy Ulrich gave us.'

Seated pensively at his desk he smoked a cigar, and then gave up waiting. 'Ah, but of course.' He crushed out his cigar in a mortar. 'My angel,' he wrote hastily on the second sheet of his note-paper—the brown stain of a cup of coffee rendered the first unusable—'I must leave you this evening in a hurry for Goerres, where poor Fuchs is waiting for me. I'll write from there. Your H., who loves you above all.'

Having written this black lie he saw gleaming once again, under damp hair, a hesitant eye.

He took off his shoes, went to put the letter under his wife's night-cap, and laid on it the pencil appropriated from Fuchs, a pencil closely resembling, he now noticed, those used by Mme Friedrich to annotate her scores. Hastily he did some light packing. He went down again to his study, his shoes in one hand and his bag in the other. The clock in the hall struck, then that in the dining room; one or two seconds later he heard the bells of the town. On the threshold into the garden Friedrich resumed his shoes and went off to the fairground. The sky was overcast, the ground black. Once beyond the lamp posts of Leopoldgasse it was hard to see one's way. Friedrich walked with arms outstretched, fearing a sudden encounter with van Aalsen and his dogs. In this way he cleared the copse between the town and the fairground. Then, before him was the open field where the circus people camped among the cages of their animals.

How to find her?

Van Aalsen had received her into his caravan with its walls of hide. Didn't his dogs sleep at the bottom of the steps? Friedrich prudently skirted the black mass of the World Beyond Belief; in the seams of its canvas there gleamed small low-burning lights. Friedrich's eyes were accustomed to the dark. He recognised, a few metres from the big tent, the massive form of van Aalsen's caravan. Its windows and door were all equally dark. He approached, uncertain. But the dogs were not there. No doubt their master was sleeping elsewhere. Happiness poured itself through all his limbs like a white star radiating out to infinity. He climbed the caravan steps, opened the door, which was not locked—honest, trusting people, these! Marvellous Child of Evil Stars! She was there, she was waiting for him in the dark. He strained his ears. She was breathing slowly, and each of her breaths finished with a painful whistle. When at last, groping, he found a lamp he could light, she emitted a little cry. And in the trembling circle of light from the lamp he held at arm's length she appeared without her hood, her black hair stuck to her temples. Friedrich laid himself down against her. His busy tongue forced itself between the lips of the Child of Evil Stars. She groaned. 'My love, my one and only love!' And Friedrich, forgetful of everything, Friedrich on fire, slid himself under the blanket of the dying ill-starred child.

☙

Dr Friedrich died that night, to all appearances in the wreck of the little ferry boat which every hour crossed the Grodden on the way to Goerres. His body was not found, any more than those of sixteen other passengers; but the inspector recalled having made him pay for his ticket, and having joked with him about the imminence of the storm. The doctor had smiled and watched for the next lightning flash. It was a storm of extreme violence and drove the ferry against the far bank a few metres from the jetty. Of the travellers who were waiting on the other side two were drowned after throwing themselves into the water to save the victims of the shipwreck.

❧

The cyclops-girl, the prisoner of the World Beyond Belief, died several days later of a sudden haemorrhage. In the space of an hour she brought up all her blood. It fell to the lot of Doctor Lehner, Director of the hospital and chief legal expert, to perform the autopsy. He was assisted by Professor Meczlaw, an anatomist whose wax models were on sale as far away as San Francisco, and Dr Fuchs, whose curiosity had been brought into the open by the double death. Was it not of her, this girl-monster, that Friedrich's last words had been spoken?

He had her under his eyes the whole time of the autopsy. The cyclops-girl did in fact have only one eye, almost central in her face, the other, never having been well formed, being hidden under a fold of skin. Lehner found she had only one kidney, and her lungs were almost entirely eaten away by tuberculosis. 'We have here an extreme case of. . . .' muttered Lehner. Meczlaw made a drawing and Fuchs held his peace. The poor girl's stomach was full of black blood which she had been unable to stop swallowing. But in the bloodless lining of her uterus, where the haemorrhage had been triggered, Lehner found, almost by chance, a round, shiny object which he placed on the rim of one of his dishes, beside the dead girl's liver. Meczlaw raised his eyebrows, and Fuchs, whose cheek still preserved the memory, sweet, burning and bitter, of the lips of Friedrich's widow, pressed against him for too brief a moment, Fuchs, thunder-struck, recognised the wedding ring of his friend.

# FOX INTO LADY

## I

KEIKO is lying in the grass of the narrow garden, her head against the cement wall, her mind a blank, when she is seized again in the pit of her stomach, in the place where, she imagines, her ovaries are located, or perhaps her Fallopian tubes, she doesn't know which, by incomprehensible pangs of pain. They come and go, and have been twisting in this part of her body, soft and defenceless, since the small hours of the morning. Feeling her abdomen with both hands Keiko detects a growth the size of an apricot which rolls beneath her fingers and which appears half an hour later (she has fallen asleep again and re-awakened) palpably larger.

She goes back into the house. The passage from light to shade makes her heart falter. Everything is green within and the interior of the house seems to her tapestried in a huge net. She thrusts her finger into the net, chokes with disgust, then pulls herself together. These specks moving before her eyes, these trembling limbs, they are nothing. Once in the bathroom she has already recovered her spirits—low as they are at this end of a summer in which the wind has never ceased, or the bad news. She is leaning on the rim of the bathtub when another sharp pain catches her. She sits on the floor panting. An iron tube is passing through her pelvis, from the labia to the uterus. A

20

sudden spurt from this scorching passage of hot black blood, clots that the tormented girl could almost squeeze in her fingers to break them open; then in the thickness of the discharge there is formed something with a head and limbs. 'Lick it, lick it,' says an instinct which Keiko in her terror cannot hear; 'it is the fruit of your belly.'

Keiko washes it clean in the hand-basin. It is a little animal with brown fur, the size of a mole, and its eyes are not yet open. Pensively she washes the private parts between her legs while the little creature mews in the basin. What is she to do? What to make of this blood-smeared apparition? Keiko opens the bath taps, fills the tub to the brim with water that is rather tepid than hot, and lies down in it. At the end of an hour of lassitude she finds the misshaped birth still alive at the bottom of the basin, and trying to escape from it by means of paws with transparent claws. Before her sister can return—the two girls are sharing the house, which had been the home of their dead parents—Keiko has time to find in the downstairs lumber-room a box in which to shut the animal away; her idea is to let it die of hunger. Then she waits for her sister, sitting in the drawing room with the television switched off, and sees in her mind's eye the animal's tiny mouth, its eyes protruding beneath lids still gummed together, its soft ears. The sun enters through the top of the window and falls slanting on the floor-boards. When it reaches the foot of the wall her sister returns and wakes Keiko who has fallen asleep, her back to the television, and has dreamed fitful disturbing dreams of landscapes with towering rocks that scraped the low-flying hunting aeroplanes.

Night comes. Keiko goes down to see if the creature is dead. It is not. Lying in a corner of the box it trembles when Keiko touches it, yet appears to have grown bigger. Returning to her bedroom Keiko feels fear. The new-found gaze of the beast, limpid and black, sticks to her heels, and climbs back up her leg to the damp nest from which it emerged.

21

Her sister is asleep, her right hand over her breast. Very softly she snores; from time to times her lips sketch a mimic sucking. Keiko looks at her as she sleeps. Terror so grips her muscles that she is without power to move. For a moment she imagines that she is no more than a skin stretched over a huge, formless, palpitating amoeba. The skin bursts; Keiko returns to protozoan disorder. Neither in the next few days nor in those that follow does Keiko tell her sister of this creature so unexpectedly come into the world. The box is hidden in a cupboard off the hall which her sister, Keiko thinks, will never open. Nor does she speak to anyone else of this unnatural birth. The desire is not lacking—but the words?

The first day, having left the house without so much as visiting her beast in its infancy ('If only it would die!') Keiko is gripped at midday by a nameless panic. Her sister will have found the animal, she will have taken it to the vet, the apparition will have been registered officially. 'But this little monster,' says Keiko grasping her hair in both hands, 'this blood-sucking witchling wants our skin.'

Her sister has done no such thing. Returning at lunch time in a state of collapse Keiko takes her beast from its box. It has gained strength. Its fur, softer now, is growing out light red. It has no teeth as yet; nor, so far as Keiko can tell, has it any inclination to cry.

Keiko returns to the garden. The sky is uncertain. The creature, probably, is puling and twisting in the darkness of the cupboard, far from the woman who gave it birth. Keiko likewise is restless. She would like to go to bed, to sleep—no, she goes out again to work. In the street she stops, a dart planted under her heart. What is the beast doing in the dark? What is in its mind? How is it nourishing itself? Has it perhaps crept back unobserved to its nest, and is it devouring Keiko from within?

II

The second night of her strange calamity Keiko falls asleep numb with fear. Her sister is away in Yokohama till the end of the week. In the hall close to the cupboard where the creature is living out its agony there hangs a smell of sweat turning to gangrene. But Keiko, terrified of finding the creature more vigorous, provided now with claws and teeth, will not open the door. She cooks spaghetti, sits up late watching television, allows a dark languor to turn her bowels to water; then goes out, vacillating, into the garden, breathes the air, puts off the moment of going to bed. The moment comes all the same. And Keiko wakes up in the middle of the night, a weight on her chest, in her mouth a taste of tainted food. By the light of her bedside lamp she sees on the skin of her ankles and calves the marks, hardly darker than the surface of her skin, of the greedy lips of the creature now launched at last upon the world.

She gets out of bed, rigid from head to foot. The animal is not in her bedroom. It has escaped out of the cupboard, that is all, that is as much strength as it has acquired. Keiko searches for it all through the house, cupboards, attic, under the furniture, and in the little garden. The beast has returned, Keiko prays, suddenly furious, to its foul beginnings. Through the hour that follows, seated in the chair she often leaves leaning against the wall of the house, she listens to the thunder of the motorway and the stray sounds of the neighbourhood. Two or three houses away a raucous discussion breaks out between students; somewhere else they are trying to start a car; a small dog yaps. Keiko recalls how her elder brother (he has been in the north for two years) went out into the garden to sleep under just a blanket. 'It was a starry sky,' thinks Keiko, 'a night that no one could fear.' Vain memories; the fear returns even though the sky is clear and the garden small and without hiding-places. Keiko sees passing shadows denser than they should be. Going back into the drawing room she seats herself before her mother's shrine and addresses to her a useless prayer. What can she, dead as she is, do against this beast that is now on the loose? Keiko looks at its scratches on her legs; no, the beast is not in the land of the dead.

Perhaps it has been run over by a car, or perhaps, this is her secret hope, it has drowned in the sewers. Her sister is back from Yokohama. The marks fade away. Keiko spends a night at the Hotel Vukuran in a red bedroom with her lover, who is a divorcé living in Kamakura. But although he strokes the underside of her breasts and works upon her tenderly, Keiko bites her lips and weeps tears of misery when his back is turned. The passage of the beast has seared what for the time being she calls her inner parts. From the window of the room nothing can be seen except one of the walls surrounding the commercial centre, and to the right of it, the end of a neon sign which Keiko deciphers and reconstructs as 'Tobacco Baruder'. 'The beast knows, it smells the fire,' thinks Keiko, squeezing her legs, 'it knows where to find me.' The question keeps recurring: has the creature come back to rest in the girl's womb? Is it not consuming her in an evil feast, inch by inch?

'I have hurt you,' whispers the man, seeing Keiko arched up, with her veins standing out. 'It's not that at all', Keiko would have liked to say, shrugging her shoulders and breathing slowly to calm the frantic beating of her heart. She stays silent. The man, not without uneasiness, takes her in his arms again. She suffers less this second time. The man, as is their usual custom, goes off to take the early train, leaving her asleep. At about seven o'clock, before going to work, she spends a long time washing her pubis and the lips of her vagina. She strives with the aid of a mirror to see what has been scorched. Nothing. Then the creature, whether it has ventured to creep back into Keiko or is leading a half-wild existence in the marginal areas about the town, falls slowly into oblivion.

III

Comes November. Keiko returns home one evening by Meguro, along the river which laps coldly against its enclosing walls. She looks at the movement of the water under the trees. Her fear returns, she could not say why. The river flows unbroken. She halts on the bridge, and her eyes sweep round in search of what can have awakened a fresh alarm. She enters the supermarket at the station to buy octopus and instant noodles; then takes the metro with her anxiety unabated, though it is still broad daylight. Her sister being again in Yokohama the house is empty and dark. Keiko switches on a light in every room and mortise-locks the door, something she ordinarily does not think to do. For the last four months she has been carrying a child of which the man from Kamakura is the father. She learnt this only this morning; he does not yet know. In point of fact she asks herself with an increasing melancholy if she has to tell him. Not that she is afraid he will cease to love her; rather, she thinks as she enters the garden, it is of the child that she is afraid. What will it be? At the bottom of the garden, which is bordered by three gloomy cedars, the darkness, into which she stares unthinkingly, causes her to tremble. She is now swimming in a sea of anguish which tosses and batters her. The darkness of the night is streaked with threatening lights. Waiting in shadow, more and more distinct, is a creature with the form of a fox—a vixen, rather, for its limbs are slender and its muzzle delicate. And this animal, the moist smell of which comes now to Keiko's nostrils, growls and whimpers, and in the middle of its inarticulate cry pronounces with horrible distinctness the word 'Mother'. Keiko puts out her hand towards the beast, motions angrily to drive it away. The word is repeated. She bolts into the house, slides shut the glass door and slams down the catch. The beast approaches. Keiko can see only the depths of its eyes shining with a yellow-orange light on the other side of the glass. She draws the curtain and sits with her face towards the animal she can no longer see. It scratches at the door and whines; then 'Mother' in a voice that is thick and inhuman.

Seated in the middle of the room Keiko hears the slightest sounds of the vixen. Her thumb and index finger at her throat count the beats of her heart, the pace of which subsides as the beast grows calmer and withdraws. But that is not for long. It returns to rub against the fastening of the window, against the walls and shrubs; it barks. She ought to leave the house, but an insurmountable weariness has seized Keiko. She gets as far as the front door, which gives onto a small flagged courtyard; but at the moment when her fingers touch the door handle she knows that the beast is waiting for her, plaintive and ubiquitous.

She puts her hands flat on the door. 'What do you want?' she asks. 'Mother,' comes back the voice. 'Never,' replies Keiko, choking with horror and fury.

At the door into the garden on the other side of the house there are the same sounds, the same exchanges. 'The night is multiplying the monsters around my house. I'll wait for morning; then they'll have disappeared.'

She goes upstairs to bed, her knees like cotton. She recalls for the first time without the veil of self-deception the day the beast was born. It is not so late. She calls her lover (he is on a business trip to Tomakomai) to talk to him about that child that is on its way; but there is no reply and she puts down the receiver without leaving a message—her broken voice, she is afraid, will betray her. She lies on the bed fully dressed, she unbuttons her shirt, she places both hands on her belly and her fingers discover again this object which more resembles something invertebrate than an embryo, an amorphous mass with languid movements floating in her bowels. She falls asleep in the familiar hollow of that jellyfish to which the darkness gives gigantic proportions; she returns to consciousness aching. The beast to which she gave birth in the past summer, now large and pale, is stationed at her threshold. It comes forward. Keiko backs off and falls to her knees, lips compressed. The beast has become the size of a wolf. Its hair is long, its limbs are powerful. It circles round Keiko and nudges her with its paws and muzzle, but without biting or scratching. Twice it forces its huge groin between its mother's thighs, which it could have opened wide with a single snap of its teeth. As it does this it pants and grunts with pleasure. Keiko tries to rise to her feet. The giant vixen reseats her with a heavy blow of its back leg.

Presently the body of the girl is in the stomach of the beast, and her spirit flutters briefly between the separated pieces. The vixen leaves the house and stalks through the streets under the cover of the night. Sounds travel through its fur, skin and intestines, which the scattered parts of Keiko would still be able to hear: sounds of car-engines, of asphalt brushed by wheels, of human voices, but also of the puissant heart-beats of the animal, the creaking of its bones as it trots in the ditch beside the road. Then fallen leaves, the smell of decaying undergrowth, earth scraped by the monster. What had been Keiko succeeds at last in dissolving itself in the recesses of the gigantic beast, which, wearied by its running is now gone to rest in a hole in the forest. Winter is on its way. It will sleep and, alone of its species, bring forth young at the return of the spring.

# THE OLD TOWPATH
*for Blandine Longre*

## I

ADA'S parents forbade her to follow the path which went from the city to the motorway and which crossed some makeshift marinas along the River Ouse, where moored only unlawful boats. On those boats dwelt fearsome, silent watermen, their mangy dogs and sullen wives. Girls had drowned there, body and soul. And when they had survived they had married down the towpath, a fate probably worse than death. They would skinny-dip at night in the brownish Ouse and offer their breasts to evil boatmen, who'd knock them down and bite them and make them bleed and moan—thought Ada. For there were children on the verminous bank: born of flesh, certainly, not of the muddy Ouse.

A weedy road begat the path, a weedy road that marked the end of the city; at night there roamed more rabbits than cats. The watermen would go after both—deftly stoning them for their flesh and fur, which they'd offer, amongst other spoils, at local jumble sales. The child Ada had lived first near the city walls and knew nothing of the waste land. Then a third sibling came—there was already a younger brother—and they all moved into a small house on Cross Lane. From Ada's room one could see the city and the spires and the dark buildings of the main station. The unseen river ran on the left. Ada often dreamt of a swollen Ouse flooding the basement and the street; Red Cross barges would feed lost families.

Cross Lane was a rambling thoroughfare joining Great Southern Road and a gravelled lane that led to the city. Because of the traffic, young children were not allowed to play on its pavements and favoured the gardens, an intricate patchwork of smaller and bigger nations without common rules. Ada and her brothers would go to the Fishers but not to the Barnleys, who eventually moved out and were replaced by the childless Perkinses. Late at night, in summer, the languid Mrs Perkins would chain-smoke at the rear end of her garden and for hours chat on the phone with a man—her lover, said Juliet Fisher. The girls, hidden in the bushes of Juliet's garden would linger in the warm, pungent vapours of Mrs Perkins's cigarettes, and listen to her uneasy banter. The Fishers moved as well—little Ada was devastated by the loss of Juliet: then came the Burnsides. He was never there; she, a harried, pallid Chinese woman, spent the whole day chasing her two fat toddlers. Ada ceased mourning Juliet and befriended the Sommerville twins. They lived in a big house not far from Great Southern Road. Ada then reached twelve and her body grew: a bad surprise, an undesired change. She was banned after this from the gardens—or rather she left in brooding exile. Games and chats would bore her; she locked herself in her room, in the basement—there was a playroom, a ping-pong table, crates and broken bicycles. She would lie on the floor and let bandits take hold of her porous mind. They would come at night, plunderers and killers that they were. Fires and earthquakes followed in their wake. The desirable floods she had designed in her early days had turned into dire streams; familiar corpses were flung at the foot of her bed. Half-sleeping, she saw their bloated faces and could even tell their names. Ada herself suffered a thousand defilements at the hands of the invaders. They would sit on her breast, break her bones and grasp at her eyes with blackened fingers. At night, before they came, she would sob and bite her own flesh—and wait. There were black and yellow marks on her arms but no one in the house ever saw them—she would wear long sleeves and dab her skin with ink and Mercurochrome. No one knew about her turmoils, which she slowly turned into painful ecstasies. The bandits who came and skinned her alive every night, the pirates who threw in the reddened river the disfigured bodies of her parents and siblings were more dear to her now than their hapless victims. She'd scratched her thighs raw to put them on her scent. The best blood they had was when she'd menstruated and painted her lips and cheeks in proud disgust.

CR

The pirates lit huge suns on her bedroom ceiling and, laughing, fed on the dismembered Ada. Her orphaned soul turning into a grey-white owl, she fluttered around the stars and saw herself lying on the black, sharp rocks of a tropical shore—skinned by the avid seamen, roasted on the heated stone, swallowed muscle by muscle. The cannibals would leave her eyes for the end and banquet on her tongue and cheeks. Having been eaten alive a hundred times, Ada grew sick of the secret pirates. For nights and nights she struggled to expel from her room the innumerable guests she had so recklessly invited. She did not get her flesh back, though, or so she thought. Sea vultures and skuas had cleaned her melancholy bones when the assassins had left. In secret wonder she spied on her parents and siblings: why could not they see through her? *I'm dead, I'm clean, I'm fleshless.* She had been taught the art of lying, possibly her only ability, in the gardens, years ago: wiser girls had seen to that. When she eventually left her infamous bedroom, she tried and feigned to be alive. And soon she followed, although it was still forbidden, the path which led to the River Ouse and then, more or less, the track of the old towpath. One of the older girls was her cover. 'I'm off to see Jenny', would say the transparent Ada, throwing her parents off the scent. She would leave through the gate at the rear of the garden, as was her wont the summer before—a season dead and buried under heaps of Adas, boiled and quartered by their cruel friends. Jenny was a willing accomplice. She needed young Ada's company to cycle along Cross Lane, till they reached the gravelled track which led to the city's flowered battlements. At the crossroads Jenny met up almost every day with her first lover, a boy from Wellington Crescent. To begin with, Ada would sit nearby and watch them kissing till they were sweaty and dishevelled, eyes and teeth glinting. They dared not go any further. The flesh of their arms was throbbing. By the end of the summer Ada could not take their passionate giggling any more, nor the sight of their hungry tongues flashing from their lips, licking, mating, gloating. Thus she deserted the pair one afternoon, an undue rage distorting the beatings of her dead heart. Or was it really dead then? She knew better, she thought, and did not marvel at the amount of blood it now spluttered through arteries and veins. The path went along the high wall of an invisible estate—the mayor's daughter's, some said. Thugs had covered it with skulls and swastikas in smudged black paint. Ada, swallowing her childish tears, found an empty beer bottle and broke it against the wall. The gritty sound awoke her to clearer feelings. What came after was a wide open field of thick flowerless weeds with pale grey-green leaves, carved and powdered as by a fastidious hand. She did not walk through the field, fearing its multitude of thorns. Down the field, there stood two grim square houses, the watermen's quarters. From the weeds shot up a large velvety dog, its tail between its legs, which neither growled nor barked. There was not a waterman in sight: all gone on the river on some errand, thought the disappointed Ada. The dog stopped a few yards from her, sat and leered at her, its chops curled up, panting in the manner of her vanished pirates. She walked past it, her body taut, her lips sealed, her hands tucked deep in the pockets of her skirt. *I'm not afraid.* The dog when she looked back was licking its soft hairless belly. Ada entered the shadows between the two shacks, lined with plastic bags, broken toys and tins, things the boatmen fished from the Ouse and sold together with rabbits' skins. Further on, Ada reached the old towpath. On the other side, the bank was steep; two red cows languidly brushed off the flies. The path plunged into low, livid copses—the dusty shadow of the city ebbing with each step—and the boughs which gently scratched Ada's head grew greener and brighter. The river was running nearby, solemn sparkles gleaming on its brown, oily surface. Ada saw a barge coming upstream; stricken by a sudden fear, she leapt behind a dark shrub. But on the deck of the barge which slowly went by her, there was not a living waterman, not a child, not even a dog. A small mast bore three red triangles fluttering merrily in the wake of the ship. *The pirates are hiding*, she thought; two hands seized her by the waist.

## II

The hands were soft and quiet. They patted Ada's back, her shoulders and nape. The unflinching Ada eventually eluded them and turned around. There stood a middle aged woman in a mauve dress, a waterwoman, judging by her dry features and tanned skin. 'Will you come with me, girl?' Ada tucked her arm under the woman's. 'I saw you alone on the path; I thought maybe you too were coming.'

Ada nodded. They walked in silence along the towpath, in a thickening wood the light of the sun reluctantly pierced. The woman strode behind Ada whose body was, under the effect of a dazzling fear, slowly filling with a black and thick liquid. Splitting her bones and guts, fear, though, was turning again into secret pleasure—this was when the woman reached out and touched her cheek, which she did a few times with incredulous awe.

Beyond the woods there was a broad field of undefined use, sheltered from the traffic and noise of the main road by a battlement of reeds. Animals had lived there, one could tell from the dried-up tracks. A huge shed, white walls adorned with wild, gaudy stories from the city, stood between the old towpath and the river's bank. Never in her life had Ada walked so far from home. The irregular rumour of the traffic did nothing to slow the shrieking of her heart. 'Ah, let us stop,' said the woman in a low moan. Quick and silent, she overtook Ada. Her arms closed on the girl and she added, with averted eyes: 'This is our church.' *Why be afraid?* wondered Ada. *I have already died a hundred times.* Shivering, eyes dancing in their sockets, she followed the woman into the shed. It was not dark under the iron roof. The dry light of a few naked bulbs hanging from the beams fell on the grey floor. Folding chairs, a dozen of them, were arranged in a circle; in the middle there was the flat, dull lid of a closed trap. 'We are not late,' said the woman, although most of the chairs were already taken. Were they all of them water people, those patient believers in the woman's church? One of them, a man carrying a bunch of lilies, had a faintly familiar face. They both sat with the others, and the silent congregation kept on waiting. Fear abandoned Ada as she peered at their half-hidden, brooding faces. They were from the city. The man with the lilies she had seen several times in front of the school—the father of a pupil, a teacher maybe. A young woman holding a toy guitar on her lap was, Ada knew for sure, a clerk at her parents' bank. The man with the lilies was sobbing without restraint, tears darkening his grey-blue shirt. Later on, he tucked the bunch of lilies under the chair and set his glittering eyes onto Ada.

CR

Did Ada sleep, her head on the woman's shoulder—did she dream, a rare occurrence under her parents' roof? Short black flames sprang under her skin; the pirates were back at their evil doings, turning against the girl the ardour of her own blood. Now the trap had been opened and a rumour of subdued hope throbbed around the gathered expectants. The woman in the mauve dress stood up and so the others. The woman slowly lowered her hands on Ada's shoulders, made her turn and marched her towards the trap. Ada, flesh still burning under her skin, went down the steep stairs of a hidden ladder, stumbled and fell on her knees next to a wide basin, filled up to the rim by a chalky water where swam loose debris. Ada felt nauseous. The underground room smelled of rotten flesh. The expectants squatted round the basin. Did it slip under their skin as well, this shivering scent of corruption, buzzing with myriads of flesh-eating gnats? She dared not look at them and ducked down, elbows close against her hips. Were they praying? A mumble went round and round the basin. Faces blackened with unrest; fingers were bitten, hair pulled by twisted hands. Bodies rocked slowly; heads thudded against the wet stone of the basin. Ada, eyes closed, heard names and sobs. Then the woman nudged her and showed her the basin. What should one see there? What lifeless fragment of muscle and bone, what orphaned eye, what awful memory of past happiness? Ada cried and caught some tears in the fold of her sleeve. Those were clear tears she shed without great sorrow while the convulsed expectants were looking at her. The man threw the lilies in the basin. Flies gathered on the dank rim.

CR

Ceaselessly crying Ada went back by the towpath. The woman in the mauve dress had seen her to the door of the shed; she had stroked her cheek with her left hand, the fingers of which she had then licked with a sigh. *Do my tears smell, then, and of what, and of what?* The woman, still silent, had vanished through the trap. Alone in the shed Ada had seen one of the walls gaping and giving birth to a wheel of colours which spun and gave a faint whistling sound. A like wheel the pirates of yore would have embedded in the ceiling of her room, so that she could rest and rejoice a while before the onslaught. Oh cruel deserters, traitors! Her tears did not wash the smell away. Night came and in her bedroom she could almost see the odour slithering on the floor, the stale reek of the holy basin. Seated on the edge of the bed, Ada waited for it to wreck anew her entrails and blacken them to the bone. *Wherever I go now the living will hate me and shun me in their daily doings.* And although the house had been shut up for the night, she got dressed, went down the hall and out into Cross Lane. On her return from the Ouse no one had questioned her; she had had dinner with her brothers and had watched a film with her mother, during which they had both fallen asleep. Her father had woken them and had carried his daughter to her room. *But I have lied all the same and disobeyed, and am walking on a path they forbid.* Kind they, tender they. And yet she went to the end of the lane, her stride all the stronger since the lights from the streetlamps did not leave a corner of shadow on the pavement. Ada was perfectly alone and never turned around to make sure of it. From behind the trees which edged the lane, soon to turn into the towpath, sparkled other streetlamps. Crossing the weedy field where thorns scratched her ankles till they bled, she heard the boatmen's dogs growling, and saw the walls of their shabby houses. Night had travelled down to her limbs and now she could hardly feel them; the path was so dim that she had to lift her lifeless hands and grope at the bushes. Between the houses and the marina, she let herself be bullied by darkness. It knocked her breasts and bit her nose and tried to rip her belly open. *Don't, don't!* Shreds of her body were swallowed by the night, leaving gaping holes where she could have lodged her fist. Night at last left her panting on the bank of the Ouse. Ripples of water were gleaming in between the barges. Not a single light at the barges' windows, not a single waterman asleep on the deck, not a single siren paddling in the muddy Ouse. The bruised Ada went down a small ladder aboard the *Blue Star*—or so the name was painted—which was as empty as the others, as empty as the watermen's houses. She sat on the edge of the deck and left her legs dangling, and gave vent to vague, choking regrets. *Deserters, deserters all!* Then came a weariness, the like of which she never had experienced. Her blood felt thin and dull. *Who will come, who will love me?* A tingling layer of pain descended on her skin. Her flesh-eating pirates had gone forever and with them sweet memories of pain, burning suns, charred limbs—her own, she knew, she remembered . . . and then no more—on the shore, offered to the sea gods. She stumbled back to the path, looked at her arms and legs, and touched her face in the grey darkness— intact and whole. It was a bitter track which took her through the woods and into the open fields, next to the motorway. There stood, in a faint orange mist reflecting the lights of the road, the faithful church—the church of mourning parents, Ada now knew.

*I will open the hatch and step down the ladder.*
*And descend, if I may,*
*In forgetful waters.*
*I have grown out of life.*

# THE OPENING

THEY had arrived at the beach after losing themselves among the dunes, which at this time of year were white with flowers. Little scuttling animals caused runs of sand down the slopes. The radio for a long time had taken over from conversation; it broadcast incomprehensible songs that eventually put to sleep infant and dog alike. A few yards before the beach, on the edge of the road, three youths, very warmly clad, were staring, hands on their knees, at the two young women who climbed down from the mobile home and stretched themselves. They kept silent, however, eyelids lowered over pupils contracted to pinpoints by the excess of light.

'Okay with you here?'

Mag's glance took in the dizzying sparkle of the sea, the gravel of the parking area down in the cutting where the road ended, the grey wall of the café, and lastly the stupid smiles of the kids sitting on the sand. At first, seeing them in the distance, she had thought them older and vaguely menacing; but they were just three high school pupils playing truant. There were two girls with blue eyes, heavily made up, and a boy who very conscientiously stubbed out his cigarette on the edge of the road before disposing of it in a bottle of beer that was still half full.

'English, do you think?' said one of the two girls with a chuckle. 'Anglaises, hein? *English*?'

Leaning back against the camper Mag let the warmth flow down from her forehead to her breasts under her shirt. Em woke up the baby. The dog barked. The metal of the mobile home vibrated to an unfamiliar kind of music. And the sea? Yes, every wave of the nearby sea caused a tremor in the air and the solid bodies.

They spent the day on the beach, the child in the shadow of a large sun-shield, and the dog beside her, asleep most of the time, but waking in starts to go and paddle in the warm pools. The three kids came back in the afternoon dressed for the beach. Mag did not see them arrive, having gone for a walk round the muddy harbour. The beach was vast; neither to the north nor to the south could any end be seen. But it was interrupted by streams from the land and large black posts, and Mag thought she could also make out skiffs or small fishing boats drawn up a mile or two to the south.

The harbour at midday was even more deserted than the beach. Little birds similar to sandpipers were running over the seaweed seeking a meagre livelihood. Mag also saw a larger wading bird with a black body and red wings that was drawing out of the sludge an endless worm. At her approach this bird flew off with a cry so plaintive that Mag, thinking of the child, felt a pang of sympathy for it.

ଔ

They had come from England, spending several days on the journey and sleeping every night beside the road; they avoided the towns, rather from preference than from necessity. There was a skylight in the roof of the mobile home, and from the upper bunk, where Mag slept, you could see a sky streaked with magnified stars—when stars were visible. They fed themselves on tinned foods, packet soup and condensed milk, the baby as well as the women. There had been stars and comets the last night before the beach, and aeroplanes flying so low and frequently that Mag realised at last that the stopping place they had chosen was two fields from a landing strip. Em and the baby slept uninterruptedly but Mag, in order to subdue her body's reluctance to sleep, was obliged to have recourse to hypnotic games with her mobile telephone. She fell asleep eventually when the last aeroplanes had passed, serpentine after-images gleaming under her eyelids.

Then came the sunken road with hedges which nearly met above the camper, and trees whose branches plucked at it.

'Odd country,' said Em; Mag was driving, and taking care not to scrape the sides.

'What's that?'

They found a frequency which broadcast only music, then lost it, and in time came to ignore the crackling, preferring it, perhaps, to the silence that filled the cabin once the radio was reduced to silence.

*With this haywire radio we will go to the end of the world.*

℣

The smell of the mud was going to her head. Seaweed was rotting there and lengths of rope, along with crabs by the thousand, mussels and other shells scooped clean by the birds. Mag kept to the edge, one foot on the seaweed, the other on the sand, which was already burning hot. Dwarfish horses grazed peacefully in the field at the end of the harbour. Mag slept for fifteen minutes, or maybe thirty, in the shadow of the animals' shelter, an erection of corrugated iron. She was woken by a sound like whinnying, but the horses had all disappeared.

She went back to the beach with the idea that a bird larger than the rest had flown over the harbour and was going to return and strip them, the two of them, of what they held most dear, the infant and the dog. Or perhaps of something else which she could not bring herself to name. Rounding the dunes she saw the white and blue parasol; the dog ran to meet her. Em, beneath the parasol, was giving the baby milk. It was just after four o'clock; in her absence the beach had come to life. A pick-up spilt out some fifteen excited school kids; scuba-divers passed in black wet-suits, tridents in hand. Then families with huge dogs that made Sparks retreat in terror to the pole of the sunshade. Sparks was a charcoal grey mongrel, still young, lazy and a joker. The over made-up girls who had formed the committee of welcome had a watch dog of their own too, a wolf-dog of unnatural darkness which paced to and fro before the sunshield, growling while they sunned themselves at a distance of ten or twenty yards from Em and Mag. Of the boy there was now no sign. Then Em went to splash herself, the baby in her arms The wolf-dog dug in the sand. One of the girls, red from the sun, gave it a sharp smack on the back.

'Don't be afraid, it's gentle. *Faut pas avoir peur. T'as peur?*

'No, I'm not afraid.'

'I'm not afraid'—that was a lie.

'What's he called, your dog? *Quel nom?*'

CR

In the evening clouds appeared on the horizon and changed slowly to orange and then to blazing red. Glory showered down on the high sea. Em and Mag bathed the child in the wash-basin of the camper van. The tide had come in so fast that the beach now seemed black with people. Men, women, children were packed between the water's edge and the dunes. Here and there fires were lit. Em did not want to picnic on the beach; she felt tired. They went for a sandwich at the little café by the parking space, the sleepy infant lying against Mag's shoulder, the dog on its leash. From the café all they could hear was the singing getting louder, and fireworks that fizzled and then exploded.

'There's a lot of people on the beach,' ventured Em when the waitress brought their order.

'It's Saturday,' the woman replied. 'And, specially when it's a fine afternoon, people come to spend the evening. They have fun.'

She too was speaking slowly, taking care to be understood.

'And you?'

'Oh, when I was younger, yes. Now I take the car and go home. We shut for the night.'

The woman lived in the village three or four miles away.

ᘓ

It was like a safe haven in this café, swimming in the odour of coffee and fried fish. Mag would have gladly slept between the tables. At ten o'clock the woman shrugged her shoulders and began to stack the chairs. The sky had clouded over again when they returned to the camper. A band of green above the sea marked the end of the day. *We should go and see the sun rise on the other side of the country. It's possible if we start now.* Em had brushed her teeth without saying anything; Mag had heard her crying. Now Em was sleeping, the baby on her bosom, as often happened of late, and Mag did not have the courage to start up the engine again, though it would probably have woken no one but the dog.

ᘓ

Mag switched on the little television fixed above the hand-basin, which served also as sink, and watched without making any sense of what was necessarily a silent film. A very small man in a white shirt was sleeping under a porch. His sleeves and his neck shone in the darkness, and his suddenly startled eyes. A second miniscule personage approached him from behind, a weapon in his hand, a club, a bludgeon that he brought down on the other's skull. A gigantic eye dripping dark tears invaded the screen. Mag went out of the camper without switching off the channel or locking the door This moist eye had given her a desire to go and see the sea. She fancied for a fleeting moment that it would watch over Em and the baby.

The dog had followed her. It trotted close to her, its tail low-ered, and she had not the heart to order it back into the camper. Two other motor homes were docked beside the road, and in one of them at least people were still awake. A head with short hair passed in front of one of the illuminated windows. Mag and the dog avoided the opening that led downwards, and climbed up through the dunes to look at the sea from above and count the fires.

There were more of them now than at the beginning of the evening. Mag and the dog walked along the spine of the dunes, which was deserted. The sea was black and lacteous: but what animal secretes nourishment so sombre?

Then the dog gave a joyous bark and hurled itself towards the beach. Mag ran after it. The tide was ebbing; there was foam at its breast.

*We could give it as food to the baby. It would be better than these packet soups on this aimless journey of ours, and what are we going to do when our supply runs out?*

Once they were on the beach the sea could no longer be seen; only the big bonfires and the shadows of men and dogs.

Approaching some piles of firewood, Mag could also make out faces, bare shoulders and bottles that passed from hand to hand.

'Sparks! Sparks!'

A man stood up and took her by the arm. On the other side of the fire some dogs were fighting over a piece of wood, and among them was the enterprising Sparks. She squatted down beside the man, and he passed her one of the bottles. What she drank was neither water nor wine but a sugary kind of spirits, cheap bottled punch coco or batida. The man threw some small sticks on the fire and his friends started to laugh, and lay down on the sand. Mag was soon drunk, and when the men stood up, she did the same and followed them in the direction of the waves.

CR

They were silent now, some with cigarettes on their lips, eyes shining. They walked straight on and others joined them, some, however, hesitating and some on all fours—men and dogs. One of Mag's companions, who had furnished himself with a burning torch from the fire, dropped it presently into a warm pool where it went out with a hiss. Away from the fires beach and sea reverted to the same greyness. The dogs were now running between their legs. One of them, a gigantic beast with bristling fur, brushed so close to Mag that it nearly knocked her over. An arm held her up, then released her. In their attentions to Mag the men were quite delicate. One of them gave a kick to the dog which made it yelp and run off into the waves.

They stopped. Mag, drawing herself up, swayed backwards and forwards. The alcohol inspired her with senseless hopes. She placed her hands flat on her stomach, breathed deeply and waited.

'Look!' said a voice.

'Where?'

'Ssh.'

Those who had been running held their sides; the man who had made Mag drink took her by the waist, rested his chin on the young woman's shoulder and calmly nibbled her skin.

'Yes.'

The dogs leaped into the waves. A few yards from them a woman swimmer came out of the water, skin and hair glittering, arms spread. The men chuckled gleefully.

'D'you see?'

Mag could see. The largest dogs had seized the swimmer by her throat and forearms. Several men pressed after them brandishing sticks and broken bottles and shouting with laughter.

'You see okay?'

The man's tongue insinuated itself into her ear. He slipped both hands into her trousers and squeezed the fleshy part of her thighs. The swimmer had disappeared, buried under the pack, which more and more dogs joined.

'Are you for it?'

Mag trembled but she followed him. Below the surface of the water she saw the remains of the other woman, wounds and torn skin, bones sticking out from muscle, jaws and paws of the dogs scrabbling in her bowels, a white hand which plunged into the seaweed, parted it, and emerged gloved in blood and other matter.

'Come on,' said the man, thrusting Mag into the crowd.

ରଃ

The man accompanied Mag back to the opening that led down to the beach. Sparks followed, having soaked himself in the same water. Mag was weeping. For a moment she had seen herself under the hounds, dismembered in her turn; then Em in her place, and finally the infant. At the foot of the dunes they looked back. Between the wood-piles and the waves men and dogs were passing to and fro, full of joy.

 C3

Em and the baby girl were sleeping in the blue light from the television. Mag washed the dog in the basin and rubbed its fur thoroughly with one of their bath-towels. Before she fell asleep she heard the sounds of engines starting up and excited laughter. With the television turned off, the skylight appeared more and more distinctly to her staring eyes, and through it a greyness increasingly clear, increasingly tender and tangible, that drove away what was left to her of drunkenness and misgiving. *This is as far as we'll go.*

## MEANNANAICH
*for Xavier Legrand-Ferronnière*

'I HAVE heard tell,' said Whimbrel, after an evening passed in turning over other memories, 'of a man of Plodish who, having lost his daughter, made her come back to life by putting out mirrors in the house where she had lived.'

'Tell us,' said Innes; their other recollections were beginning to make him yawn.

'I think I know the story,' said Fellowes, 'but I'd be glad to hear you tell it.'

'Plodish,' began Whimbrel when the last of the four, Gissen, had closed his eyes to allow the story to pass into his sleep, 'was then just a little village beside the sea. I say "then"; but that, after its hour of glory, is what it has again become. If you go there today, once you have passed the remains of the army huts you will find things just as they were at the time of the grocer Mackay ten or twenty years ago. The shore of those northern parts is so broken that to go from one house to another—and often these houses are built at the end of peninsulas with meadows and salt marshes around them—whatever the state of the tide one has to make great detours. In those days, however, the land was not as poor as you might think and the houses of the people of Plodish were large, comfortable and warm. It was a life you would find simple. In winter everything was shut up: men and animals in houses and byres. The days were dark and short, much more than with us, and wind and rain revelled over the fields. But spring, and above all, the very end of spring at Plodish, the days of May and June! That, you must realise, was the return of Paradise. There was one day, towards the end of April, often, after Easter, when the door, one did not know quite how, would come to be standing open. A little more sun, a slightly longer light in the evening; and in the clearer skies, suddenly, the songs of birds reawakened.

'It was on the day after a day like that, however, that the daughter of the grocer Mackay fell from the bridge. I must tell you of the bridge; I must tell you of the grocer.

'The grocer of Plodish was named Mackay. At thirty, coming back from the war, he married his childhood sweetheart and took over his father's grocery shop. In the port of Plodish this was the centre of the village in every sense you can give to that phrase. Like his father before him, Mackay was a devout, quiet man. Mrs Mackay, a Morrison from Otter Bay, helped Mackay at the till and talked with the women; Mackay served more the men and the older women, who preferred him. The Mackays, as people of some substance, did not live in the village. The father had built a house with two storeys on the sea-shore beside a large meadow where they grazed their sheep and their cow.

'But Mrs Mackay died two years after the birth of their only daughter, I can't tell you how or why. Mackay didn't remarry. After a short time the waters closed, so to speak, over the memory of Mrs Mackay, and father and child forgot their grief.'

'Often', Whimbrel resumed, after a long silence for which there was no reason, 'often the child, now older—the child was called Flora—used to help her father at the shop after school. Often too she would go and play with the other children of Plodish in the recesses of the shore, on the strips of sand, on the peninsulas which the sudden tide would separate from the land. She drowned falling from a bridge that had been built some years before her birth and which, for the convenience of the inhabitants, joined two of these peninsulas together. It was just at the end of April, a morning. A man of the village who was in a boat out at sea saw something red fall from the bridge. He made every effort to go and see what it was, but he found nothing. The following day Flora was thrown up by the sea and buried beside her mother on the far side of Plodish in a cemetery which the village shared with several hamlets along the coast.'

'It is a curious place,' said Fellowes. 'The sands reach up to the bottom of the cemetery. A sculptor from the town, they say, made her a crown of roses.'

'Of roses and thistles,' said Whimbrel. 'She was a very young child. Poor Mackay seemed to recover pretty well from this second bereavement. He only, to keep house for him, took from the nearby village a girl of not more than twenty, and rather pretty. At Plodish people looked a little askance, despite the misfortune of the man. But the child was not forgotten as the mother had been. Mackay used to go to the cemetery to speak to Flora and recall faithfully the day when he had held the little drowned girl in his arms, after the women had dried her hair and put a little colour on the dreadful livid face, or that other day when the men and some very young boys had followed the child's coffin through the village street. It was borne by two relations, two uncles who lived far away. And the days too when the child was alive. He passed long months in remembering and revisiting in this way the child's tomb. On a Saturday he would stay all afternoon, and the child, for Mackay more and more alive, never sank below the surface of things.

'I've already spoken of those days of awakening after winter. It came about almost exactly two years after Flora's death that Mackay, finding himself one evening near the cemetery, heard that very particular sound that a snipe makes, what we call "drumming"; the French call it "*tambourinage*", but at Plodish it had another name that is not even in the dictionaries. It is a delicate sound not like anything else, a low sawing, a plaintive tremor in the air, and often the bird, which makes this sound with the feathers of its tail—it's a mating invitation—cannot itself be seen.'

'The people of Plodish that you're talking about call it *mean-nanaich*, actually,' interrupted Fellowes in a low voice. The others did not hear him.

'Ah, you know that do you?' Whimbrel again took up the story.

'That evening there were several of these birds drumming, and hidden, as usual, in the depths of the sky, quite out of sight. Mackay heard them with a new ear, and when he entered the cemetery it seemed to him the snipe followed. And one of them, when he was in front of Flora's tomb, made its noise and departed with a short cry.

'The following day they were there again, their sound more graceful than the day before, and more of them, it seemed to him, but even less visible. So the following Saturday Mackay brought a little pocket mirror and put this at his feet while, sitting on a square stone that always served him as a seat, he spoke to the tomb of his daughter. He wanted to see if the birds were approaching him in real truth.

'I don't know what Mackay used to say to his daughter. I think it was little stories of the day, things his customers had told him, probably also news of the children Flora had known and played with. Mackay was not too certain that his daughter heard him. The war and the deaths in his house had thrown his beliefs into confusion. But speaking to Flora always gave him pleasure and that day he saw in the mirror a cloud that was not in the sky, and the almost continuous sound of the snipe gave him the sensation of a cool hand that was stroking his cheek.

'Later, pondering uneasily on the cloud in the mirror, he thought he remembered having seen that cloud—round, flat, ragged at the edges—some other day at the cemetery. For a long time he walked in the hills round about watching for the snipe, but he did not hear them again. He sat down beside a stream to reflect on these new aspects of his trouble.

'The following day it occurred to him that his visit to Flora had been heavy with expectation. He first put the mirror on the little mound which formed the tomb of his daughter. He sat on the stone and hardly knew what to say. At the bottom of his heart he was afraid of scaring away his visitor, and if the snipe had not made themselves heard he would never again have taken out the mirror, he would have even killed in its infancy the hope that had come to him. But the snipe flew high in the sky about the cemetery and in the mirror he saw—not daring, however, to look for too long—a colour in the sky which was not that of the moment, but a greenish yellow as of late evening.

'Timidly and little by little Mackay accustomed himself to these occurences, even if he did not yet know how to mention them in his one-sided conversations with Flora. And on Sunday at church the severe sermons of the minister—you know how it is in the churches of the north—no longer awakened in him either fear or consolation. He felt himself afloat on a vast summer sea, at one with the waves and swamped, presently, by them and all their seething inhabitants. Of course, there came to him once or twice the idea he was the sport of an evil demon; but in the face of his new exultation these thoughts evaporated. He continued to hear the flight of snipe although the season for that had long passed; and day after day the mirror on Flora's tomb showed him stars, lights and clouds that were certainly not in the sky at that moment. A day came at the end of summer when he heard, without seeing them, snipe flying round his house. That was something they had never done before, from fear, perhaps, of his two dogs. He took out the mirror which he had always in his pocket, put it on the door-sill, bent over it, saw a spring sky crossed by the flight back and forth of birds. That day he sent away the servant-girl who had drawn on him the village's reproaches. This girl, who was fond of him, left with regret; she feared that in his melancholy he was longing to die alone and undisturbed.

'That was not Mackay's intention. The following day he went to the shop and kept it open, his heart beating fast, till four o'clock. Then he went to Flora's tomb and spoke to her as usual. The mirror showed him a sky that changed gradually to the violet of a misty night. Mackay heard the drumming of the snipe and a curlew called—he saw it fly above the wall of the cemetery and its open beak give out the cry. In the warm air of this summer's end many things were alive, and among them Flora, surely, said Mackay, Flora too.

'Mackay went home, set up the first mirror on the window-sill of his kitchen, then another above it, and a third slanting against the window that caused there to appear on the dark wall of the kitchen a pale, roughly outlined circle on which there moved lights that were more distinct.

'In this third mirror that evening Mackay saw a rook pass, such as often comes at bad times. Then, accompanied by the clear noise of the snipe's feathers, there passed a miniature boy whom Mackay recognised as one of the favourite companions of his daughter. With the help of his mirror Mackay followed for a moment the steps of this child, but no one and nothing came to meet him, and Mackay dared not look for long. He had lost all certainties. The night about his house fell rapidly. Round its chimneys wheeled a gull with a sombre croak—heu-heu, heu-heu. You know the cry of these birds, the perpetual moodiness they manifest. Mackay listened to it for a moment, a smile, surely, on his lips. Then he took a piece of paper and a pencil, and worked out through part of the night the arrangement of further mirrors. The task finished, he went to the sea-shore, though heavy rain was falling, threw himself on his knees, and prayed confusedly to a god who was not the one whose vengeful decrees were hammered home on Sundays.

'He slept a little, and all through the night he saw the child in red trousers walking under the rain. The following day the village people found him *distrait*, and put down the change to the servant he had discharged. He had already forgotten her. Before leaving he unhooked the various mirrors in the shop and went home, but first visited the cemetery and Flora's tomb as usual, and at the moment when he spoke to her there came to him so great a happiness that again he did not know how to tell her.

'He disposed the other mirrors round the house in such a way as to be able to see the play of things seven or eight times reflected. The last mirror, gilt-surrounded, a present for Mrs Mackay once bought in the town—threw squarely on the wall the image held by the last reflection.

'He went to bed without eating, though he had taken care of the animals—the cow was relieved of its milk night and morning, and Mackay secretly threw most of it away in a ditch behind his house—and his last act was to turn his eyes on the final mirror. Late in the night Flora passed across it. She was carrying a box. It was almost dark and she had on her winter coat, a black coat buttoned up to the chin. He did not try either to detain her or to follow her. The following night he saw her again. To tell the truth, he saw her every night at the end of that summer, then on every night that autumn, and every dark, interminable night of winter.

'Things always happened in the same way. Mackay lowered the shutter of his shop, greeted the postmaster, who closed his window a little later, set off for the cemetery and spoke to Flora. His tongue was never tied; all the stories of the day came easily to his lips. At the end of the conversation he got up saying: "So, dearest Flora, dearest girl, till we meet again."

'He understood well, he thought, that the Flora of the mirrors was not that of the tomb, but he did not imagine for an instant that the child of the night could have appeared to him unless the other, the child who was dead and yet living, knew it and authorised it. Then he went home and had supper opposite a place he had set for Flora. The bread and milk used to disappear in the night, something that Mackay naturally attributed to the child's nocturnal allies.

'After eating Mackay read a little, went to the child's room, where the servant too had slept, then felt his heart gently quickening. It was the time to go to bed and wait for the moment when Flora would pass into the mirror, and when her outline, dimmer, would appear on the wall. Sometimes this was at the darkest hour of night. But Flora always seemed to be passing in the morning, her arms full. She was going to school, that was it, she was going to school. She would stop beside the sea, shrug her shoulders, throw stones at a dog that was following her and frightening her—sometimes she would walk with head held high but sometimes smiling, and Mackay would see that little smile and smile too. Sometimes Flora would pass running; wind or rain was hurrying her on.

'Some nights she did not come. No doubt she was sick. In February there were several nights when she was absent. Mackay thought he had lost her once more, and shutting his shop, took himself to the town and returned the same day, an almost impossible feat that brought a drop of blood to his lips. He had bought a dress of Indian blue and a little girl's petticoat, which he laid out on a chair in his room. That evening he had to resist an urge to add another mirror to his arrangement, but Flora reappeared two days later, emaciated, as it seemed, her head covered with a red shawl which had belonged to Mackay's mother and which he still kept in his wardrobe. The memory of the shawl and the illness then came back to him.

'He saw her for much longer that night, for, worn out, she sat down in mid-way, and Mackay heard the snipe two or three times; they also made the little girl lift up her eyes. She gathered up some pebbles which she placed at her feet, dried her fingers on a handkerchief, which a gust of wind tore from her hand, she shivered, stood up and departed.

'But on every other day she was there. When she departed Mackay went out in the night, descended to the sea-shore and looked around him, his head empty. He no longer prayed; to tell the truth he only waited for the next night.

'So passed the winter of that unhappy year in which a whole ship's crew died in the sea off Plodish—and three families shut up their houses and embarked for the mainland. Mackay followed the funerals of the sailors and sold biscuits to the emigrants. Some days he had the radiant feeling that he held in a human cage the warm and singing bodies of all the birds of the shore.

'One morning at the beginning of April as he went out he heard the cry of a snipe, then its drumming, and he stayed a little while at the door, his eyes seeking in the sky and keeping in view the bird that swooped and soared above his roof.

'Then, without his understanding why—but the snipe must have struck against one of the chimneys or the wind had dazed it—the bird fell into his hands motionless, blood at its beak. Mackay took off his hat, made a bed in it for the bird, took several steps towards the village. Then we went back into his house, trembling all over. He went to his room, put the bird on Flora's dress, lay down, and died, that day or that night, no one knows: died in the pleasure and then in the unequalled grief of following his child along her road to the bridge, and seeing her there, a little later, beneath a fine hazy sky, slip, poor soul, under the handrail and disappear.'

# II

# Crucifixions

# PASSING FORMS
*for William Charlton*


I


BALE had chosen, pretty much at random, to spend a week at Baintree. This comprised an inn and a filling station at the foot of the mountains on the main road from Inverness to Glen Shiel; nothing more.

'How are you coming?' he was asked when he telephoned the inn.

'By bus, I think. The bus from Inverness to Portree goes past you, doesn't it?'

In summer the bus passed at least three times a day.

'There's nothing but the hotel here, you know?'

Bale knew; he was coming to do some walking.

'Alone?'

'Yes, for this once, alone,' he replied. The room was booked.

And here was the inn, just off a bend in that unending road—thank goodness unending. Bale was the only passenger to get off, the driver following on his heels to dive into the bus's hold and retrieve Bale's luggage, a green canvas rucksack. The driver murmured a good wish for his stay, and Bale thankfully went off to take possession of his room even before the bus, in a cloud of exhaust fumes, had resumed its journey from Inverness to Portree.

61

❧

Bale walked. There was really nothing else to do in these spongy mountains. The Scots have little taste for marked paths, and Bale, in his chosen solitude, had no desire to go and kill himself on peaks that were reputed dangerous. He found a little road that led through the rain to the ruins of a village. As he proceeded he kept thinking of his wife, from whom he had been divorced the year before. Next day he walked the length of another small road which took him over a pass and then down to a loch, which he crossed by two bridges that had nearly disintegrated. Between the bridges was a damp island, birches growing on it out of black soil. Bale did not wish to linger on the island. On the far side of the loch the road continued through a pleasanter piece of forest. Big funguses sprouted among the roots of the trees. Breathless, eventually, and his fingers numbed, Bale retraced his steps. He stopped two or three times beside the road and felt his legs tremble.

Never could he remember having passed through country so deserted, so devoid of men or animals. Descending towards the lake he had heard jackdaws; he had also seen some small, light-coloured birds flitting without any cry above the heather. But human beings, sheep, the herds of deer that people presumably stalked in these valleys—where were they?

Back at the inn, he lay down fully dressed on his bed, not even pulling off his walking boots. He looked at the ceiling and listened to the dull sounds his body was making. If this goes on, he said to himself, I shall find myself cracking up.

He took a shower, went to dinner, and stood himself a half bottle of Chilean wine, which blackened his tongue. There was a loud racket in the bar. A man was laughing in great guffaws like a donkey, which caused hilarity in a whole party of cyclists.

It was not yet night when he returned to his room. He lifted the sash of his window and watched the wide empty valley fade into darkness. Out of the corner of his eye, vehicles could be seen, still passing, barely audible on the main road. One night in Sutherland when he was staying with friends he had got out of bed, woken by an animal instinct. Waiting for him in a circle below his window was a herd of deer, come down from the mountains. In the end he had gone back to sleep and dreamed for half the night of things without form. He counted sheep in the peat-hags, black with peat to their necks. Then he saw himself running across the moor, shod in silver, beneath a glorious sky. A procession was approaching along the path. A young child was leading by halters a pair of young hinds with translucent ears. Bale, tears of happiness in his eyes, allowed the child to pass and dwindle into the distance, and he himself went off the other way.

ᘓ

The following day it rained at Baintree from early morning. The clouds rolled down thick to the base of the mountains. Bale had walked too far the day before; nervous twitches ran through his arms and calves. He set himself to walk along the main road, a course almost as perilous, in the prevailing mist, as to go floundering without a map through the peat-hags. Every ten seconds a car passed and, oftener than he had expected, a lorry that stirred up a blast of air. The verge, however, was broad and flat, and Bale wisely kept to it.

'This,' he said, 'is really walking for the sake of walking.' In the rain the valley lacked even the funereal charm of the preceding day. Bale first counted the red cars and the grey; then he interested himself in what was lying on the verge: cigarette-packets, bottles in glass or plastic, jars and tins for preserves, newspapers, cigarette-stubs, clothes too, a pair of gloves, even a sort of anorak that was almost new, which he was tempted to save from the ditch. He recalled the little velvet jacket worn by the child with the hinds, and wondered how far he would have been able to follow the procession, lost in the confusion of the dream. Then, lying in the grass at the foot of a stake he saw the carcass of an animal, a fawn or a lamb—a fawn, probably. There were left only the bones with a little flesh and wisps of fur. Bale, who as a child brought up in the country had seen many dead animals, asked himself when the death had occurred. He felt a shiver of cold and continued on his path, head down. 'This evening, though, I'll mention it to the innkeeper, who'll probably shrug it off.' The small black island of the previous day returned to his mind, with its marshes and their crop of sickly herbs.

'I'll go as far as Glen Dhun,' he thought, 'I'll have a coffee and a whisky, and then I'll return to the inn. Eighteen miles on a day like this—that should be enough.' Enough for what? He did not know himself. Beyond a bridge from which he had watched the brown waters of a stream flowing between rowans towards a loch, he found another dead animal, decomposing in the same posture as the first, head thrown back, feet folded almost underneath the belly. The carcass was fresher, and gave off a strong smell. Bale shrugged his shoulders and sighed. 'No, to Hell with it, I won't go to Glen Dhun. I'll go on one more hour from here and then turn back.' It was all too grey, too mournful. The valley before his eyes grew more and more sombre. He had passed the bottom of the loch, and all he could see below it were the green and brown humps of the peat; a river in spate made its winding way down the middle of the valley. There was not a bird to be seen nor a sheep. On the far side of the road large red stones were embedded in a slope of loose soil, and Bale, his knees aching, gave a brief thought to the great prehistoric forests that had once flourished here. Under their giant ferns, how much of sky would you have seen?

The rain ceased. The mist, however, continued to stream down the mountains into the hollows of the valley. He stopped at the hour he had fixed, ate the inn's sandwiches and two pieces of shortbread, and after five or six minutes he felt all over his hands and down his neck the countless small bites of the midges from the marsh. He beat the air, carefully folded his greasy papers and slid them into his trouser pocket; then he crossed the road to walk back towards the inn. He might have forced himself on to Glen Dhun and waited there for the bus, but he could not find the heart for it. He returned to counting the bottles and plastic bags.

Well before the dam at the bottom of the loch—he was still five or six miles from the inn—he saw on the green turf of the verge the white outlines of a third carcass. Poor, poor fawns, his weary spirit repeated. He put his foot on the grass, leant over, leant, and was grasped by two invisible hands that slapped him and pushed him back. The remains in the ditch were those of a child. Bale shut his eyes. The inner surface of his eyelids bristled with miniscule bones. He smacked his forehead and let out a cry. Then he went back onto the road, legs shaking, arms uplifted. The first car that saw him stopped. No doubt he could have called the inn or the police; he had a mobile telephone; but the thought did not cross his mind. 'If that fellow hadn't stopped, I should have thrown myself under the wheels of the next car.'

The kind driver bent in his turn over the ditch, then came back to Bale, lips pursed, forehead creased.

'Listen, Mr. . . .'

'Bale,' said Bale, his eyes upon a jay that fluttered from one piece of bracken to another.

'Mr Bale, we must call Inverness. We must wait here, all right?'

'Yes, certainly.'

'I'm going to call my wife, tell her that I'm delayed. My God!'

The man was called Douglas. He had a farm on Skye, a sheep-farm, he said. He made Bale get into his car, which smelt of dogs, and offered him a cup of coffee. 'It's this morning's. I made it at my sister's house, in Cromarty.'

'My ex-wife lives in Cromarty too,' said Bale for no particular reason. He could see the remains of the child reflected in the windscreen.

'What are you doing in a place like this?'

'I came for a few days' walking.'

'Where are you from?'

'St Andrews.'

As he uttered the words, he wondered if St Andrews would still acknowledge him. Did he still belong to the land of the living? Had he not seen the fawns in a dream, along with the bright blue jacket of the child?

To the police, who arrived two in a van and two in a car, after the rain had ceased and when blinding beams of sunshine were sweeping the bottom of the valley, he had to tell over again the story of his discovery and repeat the same senseless details. He was a teacher of Scandinavian languages at the University of St Andrews, he was taking a few days' holiday at Baintree for the sake of the walking. 'By yourself, out here?' The officers expressed surprise. 'That's not very sensible.'

'I see that,' mumbled Bale, on the verge of tears. The farmer from Skye had continued on his way. The police in the car took Bale back to the inn. Those in the van stayed on the verge, intending, no doubt, to fence it off with stakes and strips of yellow plastic.

'I've never seen anything like it.'

'Might have been jolted out of a car.'

'I'm not squeamish, but this. . . .'

'You're right there.'

There were two of them in the car, a flying squad, a woman police constable with short red hair whose heavy-lidded blue eyes Bale could see in the rear mirror, and on the other seat in front, half turned towards him, a massive man in a waterproof who looked something like a bank clerk.

'And people passing along the road all the time. What can you say?'

In front of the inn Bale found it all too much for him. 'I cannot stay a second longer at Baintree.' The two police officers held council in the bar. The woman blew on the wrinkled surface of her white coffee, the man had unfolded a map and was speaking in low tones, his head leaning back against the panelling. Bale went up to his little room. From the windows it was possible to see the lake and the road he had followed on the first day. He had a shower and packed, the police from Inverness meanwhile making routine enquiries about him.

'This Mr Bale, how long has he been here? Is he a regular customer? Has he come here before? When was he going to leave? Hasn't he a car?'

At the Inverness police station two inspectors were already making lists of missing children. Journalists had been to look at the verge. A sheet of black plastic covered the child. The police took Bale back to the town. He was exhausted, and slept throughout the journey.

II

The weather was fine when Bale got back to St Andrews; the sky had cleared when he left Aberdeen. He slept in his seat, bathed in sunlight. Once home he emptied his rucksack on the floor of his sitting room and went to bed. He slept for more than fifteen hours at a stretch, dreamed that he was driving a van along a bypass through an avenue of palm-trees, and then woke up in the middle of the night seized with a horror that caused him to see the dead child in every cranny of his flat. He switched on the light in the sitting room and the television, swallowed a pill he was lucky enough to find in a drawer in his kitchen, and drank two glasses of whisky. Afterwards he slept for several hours more, not waking till it was full day with a blazing sun.

During his time in the mountains several friends had written to him and others had left messages on his answerphone. He rubbed grease into his mountain boots, took a bath, went out to meet his colleagues at the Polar Bear. He had to repeat the story of his grim discovery: it had been reported in the *Scotsman* and on television and his friends wanted to hear all about it. He was happy to oblige, since summoning up his memory of the child did not cause the image of it to reappear; and though he described the incidents of the day, he said nothing of the dream that had preceded them.

On Sunday he went, as he often did, to lunch with his parents. He spoke of the main road and of the black island.

'You don't look very happy.'

'It never stopped raining.'

Neither his parents nor Bale himself had courage to dig up the bones of the little child, which gradually sank into the mud of past experiences.

∞

The same week he returned to Inverness for the inquest, and had to look at the photographs taken at the ditch. The dead child had not been identified. There was talk presently of a child of illegal immigrants, a boy aged four to six, fallen, presumably, from a lorry. The body had been lying in the ditch for three weeks, and the newspapers, which published a picture mocked up by the police, deplored the incorrigible decadence of a society which, like Saturn, swallowed up its children in mass indifference—and then, thought Bale, spat out their bones into ditches.

The following summer Bale ran into the farmer from Skye at Aberdeen Airport. Bale was heading for the United States via Iceland; Douglas and his wife were going to spend a week in Kenya.

'The child has still not been identified,' said Bale.

'Yes, so I've read. It still bothers me.'

'I'm sorry.'

Douglas shrugged his shoulders. 'And what are you going to do in Iceland?'

'Work in the archives,' Bale explained, 'at the University of Reykjavik.' After that he had a research post waiting for him at Salt Lake City.

They drank a beer in one of the small airport bars. Mrs Douglas was a good looking woman with a soft laugh that made Bale wistful.

## III

At Salt Lake City Bale for several months felt himself a new man. The day after his arrival a tornado burst upon the city. He went down into the shelter with the full complement of the Department of Scandinavian Studies, and felt the walls tremble. In the days that followed the air became so dry and dusty that he was amazed he had been able to survive for thirty years in the swampy dampness of his native Scotland.

His state of renewal lasted throughout the whole university year. He shared a house on the outskirts of Salt Lake City with two other foreign professors, two Afghans so fed up with the questions to which they were subjected about their country that they had decided to pose as Turks. Bale learnt Parsee in his spare time, and in return taught them Swedish, a language, all three agreed, that would serve them well if there was a world war. Bale flirted with a Swedish lectrice and did his best to keep out of the intestine struggles of the department fomented by the rivalry of two savages from Minnesota. He arranged an American Christmas for his parents. At New Year he went to see the snow fall in the Valley of the Gods. He wept. Now and then, in quiet moments, what he had chased from his mind came back to him: in the valley the white of the snow beneath a flat grey sky recalled the child.

In January his parents forwarded to him a letter from the police in Inverness. The child had still not been identified. Inspector Durham (Bale did not remember him) had thought for a while he had a clue; 'unfortunately the genetic testing had not confirmed it.' Bale put the letter in one of his dictionaries and went off for a drink with the younger of the Afghan professors, though he did not venture to recount to him 'the unhappy tale of Loch Baintree'. Shevar, less shy, followed the beer with three margaritas and confessed with scarlet cheeks to an unrequited passion for the lady who was chief finance officer of the University.

And Bale: was he in love with this Inge who said she was half Same, and who had bought a lamb which she kept in the garden of a house she shared with two other lecturers? Bale and Inge acquired a habit of going walking every weekend. At first Bale mistrusted himself; then he realised that walking behind Inge over the yellow dust of the desert was one of the chief delights of his new life. They went to Canyonlands, to Arches and to the Valley of the Gods. At the end of their expeditions they often spent the night in one of the three motels of Blanding, and finished their journey in the early morning. Several miles from Blanding there was a ghost town dating back, reputedly, to the

Uranium Rush. Inge and Bale visited it one night in May. They thought they saw fairy lights in a church without a roof. Inge found a passport in the name of Mary Amy Bell in the kitchen of one of the two houses that were still standing intact, and both of them felt their hearts miss a beat before they realised that the passport, being nearly new, must have been lost by a passing tourist.

'But could you imagine it, in this solitude, digging into the mountainside till your bones rot?'

Bale shook his head. They were sitting under the porch of the church; long delicate strands of cloud were passing across a half moon.

'Do you think they dug just to become rich?'

From the village, where the night wind was making the planks of the houses creak, they descended towards the bottom of a canyon through which there flowed an exiguous stream. Unseen animals rustled and chirped. Bale's eyes did not leave the dim outline of Inge's body.

'I am saved!' he said, and grasping Inge round the neck he kissed her hotly.

CR

Summer arrived, ushered in by two weeks of storm. One of these found Bale, alone for once, in the Valley of the Gods. He nearly died of fear. Lightning had split a rock at his feet. He returned tremulous to Mexican Hat, and dreamed that night of his mother and of a report he was supposed to be making, of which he had written only a third. Bale had no more fear of his dreams and their apparent coherence. From Mexican Hat he proceeded next day to Moab where Inge was awaiting him. He showed her the stone split by the lightning. Their room, number

123, gave onto wasteland over which, at dusk, swooped birds the eye could hardly follow.

'Bats, not birds.'

'Night-jars, not bats. With bats you always have the sense of spots before your eyes.'

The creatures, whatever they were, flitted to and fro in the light of the lamps.

'We go to Dead Horse tomorrow, and picnic?'

'If you like.'

'On Sunday, if it's fine, we could apply for a permit and sleep in the famous Maze. What about it?'

'If it's fine,' said Bale, remembering the storm.

They had dined off pizza and a bottle of wine beside the lake that lies above Moab. An old man with a beard was bathing fully clad in the half-light, escorted by two large black dogs.

'They are going to take him to the bottom of the lake.'

'He is a god of the locality,' said Inge, who refused therefore to swim.

ᘉ

They switched off the light, opened the window, and lay close to each other, she on her back, he on his stomach, his hand on Inge's thigh. He fell asleep at once, and dreamed that he was living in a house, some of the rooms of which he did not know. Troubled scenes ensued. He was searching for a friend in the garden, beneath a desert mountain. A path led up it, and Bale set himself to the ascent. When he reached the pass he met a tall bony dog behind which there strode impatiently a woman with red hair. Bale watched her descend towards his friend's house, or rather towards the night which was filling the bottom of the valley. 'I should have followed her.' But the woman had already entered the house.

ಅ

The next day Inge and Bale set off for Tierney's Canyon. After nearly an hour of travel, just at dawn, they parked their car by a blank signboard and walked for some time along black ground, bristling with thorny bushes, until they reached the abrupt descent into the canyon. Bale walked behind Inge, careful and sweating. They descended into the canyon in silence by a track so cleverly constructed that one was hardly aware of the drops.

What was in Inge's thoughts?

'The man yesterday, the man of the lake with his two huge dogs.'

'At night the waters of that lake become phosphorescent.'

'The people of the mountains come down there and bathe, singing mysterious incantations.'

'Undoubtedly.'

She started to laugh, shivered despite the extreme heat, yawned. The bottom of the canyon bloomed with luxuriant vegetation, and Bale, close up against Inge, wished they might never leave. But they had to continue along the path, which followed the course of an invisible stream and then plunged into a labyrinth of rocks belonging to a larger canyon. They stopped again for lunch at the mouth of Russell's Canyon. Russell and Tierney, farmers or hunters, had left behind no traces beyond their names. Bale left Inge for her siesta and went off to explore the blind recesses of the canyon which lay off their path. The walls were close together, the air was almost cool and of a green that was like blindness after so much sun. Feeling along the walls Bale arrived at a sort of sandy alcove from which all sunlight was shut off. A large grey dog was lying there which made Bale start back; dark and menacing, it caused his heart to leap. Flies stuck clustered over its eyes, its lips, its flanks: the dog was dead. Bale touched it with the tip of his foot. Then, hands extended, he groped towards the end of the alcove. Round the corner he saw the swamp which the stream was feeding, and the red haired woman with a drowned face and her arms crossed.

⊗

He ran. He flew up the slope, driven by a panic terror that could spring only from one thought: 'I manufacture dead people; I manufacture the dead.' He scraped his forehead and his knees on the rocks of the canyon. When he found Inge sleeping in the shadow of the cliff he had ceased to be himself, that new self behind which he had hidden in fear for more than a year. He woke her.

'I fell,' he said.

'I see that, poor dearest.'

'Let's go back, if you don't mind.'

They climbed back up Tierney's Canyon. He was in tears. She walked in front, turning round from time to time so that he could catch up with her.

He tried every expedient to divert his thoughts from the abyss which once more had opened at his feet. He counted Inge's steps, felt for the beating of his pulse under his jaw, and found it irregular. Imaginary insects passed before his eyes, black, born in the abyss. 'I manufacture the dead.' He had a sudden feeling that the skin of his stomach had become so thin that the slightest thing could make it burst. 'God knows what I have in there.'

'Let's stop at Moab this evening, if you'd rather rest,' said Inge when they were back at the car.

'No, I've walked in . . .' began Bale, without knowing what he was saying.

She shrugged, but her mind was not set at rest.

'We'll go to Dead Horse.'

'We could go tomorrow evening. It's almost vacation now.'

'I'd rather this evening,' said the manufacturer of dead people. His lips seemed to him full of poison and stiffer than usual.

'She knows nothing, she sees nothing, and perhaps . . .'

An ambulance slipped past them on the way to Moab. They drove back onto the road between two cliffs of red rock.

'. . . perhaps she can save me.'

Below the road a bright green curtain of trees shut off the canyon.

*But it is too late, I was wrong, it is too late to save me. I must just end by. . . .*

ℭ

His heart, how was it beating? Back at the hotel Bale took a shower and, while Inge succeeded him in the bathroom, counted up his wounds, from which the blood had again started to flow. Then he sat at the window and looked at the white desert that surrounded the motel.

They bought a bottle of wine, bread, cheese, apples, salami and a pocket knife. They left round about six thirty. The sky which had been a whitish colour, had turned blue. Two aeroplanes, followed closely by a third, made a W against it which soon flamed red in the sinking sun.

I must go away, Bale thought. Moab and its spruce shops had distracted him from his sickness, and even made him think that the woman in the canyon was only an illusion. *You never even touched her. You saw nothing but a dead dog.*

'Inge, what if I go away with you to Sweden in August? Inge?'
Inge nodded her head with a broad smile.

'There! That's a good idea!'

They arrived too late to see the sun set. They missed it by five or six minutes according to Inge, whose spirits kept rising. Being alone, they settled themselves out of the wind beside a twisted tree. Beyond it the cliff fell sheer to a bluish plateau through which smaller canyons wound like snakes. Bale thought of the dead woman and shuddered; back to him came the child too with the fawns, and futile tears rose to his eyes.

'Drink, if you feel like it, my love,' said Inge; 'I'll drive back.'

He did drink; and saw the emerging stars trace little arcs in the dark peacock sky. The bottom of the cliff had vanished in the mist of night. Inge pointed out in the far distance a black stain which she alone could see. 'Isn't that where we were this morning?' He hung his head without looking.

Later in the darkness they saw a flicker of light above the peaks of the La Sal mountains, peaceful in the night. The light came from a single cloud which swelled steadily under the curve of the sky. Bale's mind, dulled with alcohol, was almost a blank. Towards eleven they decided to go back. The wind was raising eddies of dust, and they fancied they could hear thunder.

'Last night,' Bale started to say, but Inge, her hands on the wheel, her eyes narrowed, did not hear him. He stretched his legs under the dashboard, turned his head to the side and fell asleep, resigned. There came to him this dream, final dream on the last night of the maker of death. He was riding a horse along a small grey path that wound through the countryside; the sky pressed down. Near a boundary-stone a man was seated, hat in hand, and watched him go by. Bale, bewildered, recognised his own features, his look of incredulity. He swallowed his tears and, gripping the pommel of his saddle with both hands, he directed his horse down into the depths of the valley.

# UNDER THE LIGHTHOUSE

THE bungalow stood below a road which ended in a cul de sac as it turned down towards the sea. He rented it for £100 a month; that was all it was worth, Machree, the owner, acknowledged, and not a penny more. A fence protected it from the sheep and cows, stock belonging to Machree and the other farmers on Luag. There were several hundred fatty ewes and some cows of a breed which Crane couldn't have named; their short-haired calves would grow into stocky little beasts to be butchered as veal before the end of the year.

Crane found two advantages in the bungalow: from its windows he could see the lake, the sky and even a band of genuine sea. And then it was the last habitation on the road to the lighthouse, which was accessible only by a muddy track closed to motor vehicles. But why not live in the house attached to the lighthouse, as a keeper without a lantern, a man of all work? The property of a traveller from Australia, it was in perfect repair, and for several months a year it harboured adventurous townspeople who left their hired cars on the side of the road between a disused telephone kiosk and the two dustbins belonging to the cottage. Crane could have obtained this enviable post through the mediation of the astute Machree, who knew everyone on the Peninsula and performed the duties of justice of the peace in this land without a master. Crane preferred the bungalow, however, that wart upon the moorland, and the monotonous journeys over to the Orebost Inn where he worked as barman. It was another of Machree's protégés, a skinny girl called Katie, who looked after the lighthouse, without living there. She and her brother had a little farm three hundred yards from the bungalow; their sheep were marked with yellow and those of Machree with red or blue. There were no animals at the foot of the lighthouse, which was another of its drawbacks. Crane liked the proximity of animals.

ം

The bungalow was the second house in which Crane had lived on the Peninsula—and the last, he sometimes said to himself in a vague way. For two years he had shared a flat at Orebost with the hotel cook, an arrangement which came to an end when Jim—James McPhee—departed to Glasgow. From there Crane regularly received enthusiastic postcards: 'Come too!' 'Come back, I've got room!' Crane was fond of Jim and missed their burlesque embraces, but the moors, the moors had got under his skin. He had slept at the hotel for two months, without paying anything, before finding the bungalow at more than twelve miles from Orebost. On the three days a week when he worked in the evening he came home at two or three in the morning, after having swept out the room and filled the dishwashers, which he turned on just before leaving. In winter it sometimes happened that he made his way under skies more full of stars than he had ever seen; but it is true that he had done little travelling. At the summer solstice he would see the sun rise against skies that had never been dark.

Just beyond Orebost there was a lane that led to what was said to be a Viking harbour, a long waterway connecting a sea-loch with Loch Luag. The Vikings, the story went, had dug it out in order to bring their ships into shelter from storms. On summer mornings you would see curlews and plovers there, stirred into activity by the needs of reproduction. Often Crane would wait there for the sun to rise clear of the earth, hoping sometimes, without going so far as to delude himself, that it would fall straight back again, and the world would end with this brief hiccough of a morning.

Why this absurd taste for solitude? This world here, its machines, its houses, its people—after a moment he could not stop himself from seeing the abysses between the atoms that composed them—he travelled back too far in their short history; he unravelled the threads of time, and nothing was left in existence. At the window of the bungalow, however, what could he see when he came back to go to bed? No road, no cars, no houses. In the distance, the broken coast, almost a cliff, and the white band of the uneasy sea; nearer to him, the peat and the lake.

'In all the time that is allotted to me,' thought Crane, 'this cliff will not budge an inch.'

☙

What it was that had determined his choice, Crane did not properly know. His parents had brought him up with gentle firmness. He had a sister of whom he never thought without affection. She lived in Manchester; their parents had stayed in Thurso.

'As for you,' Crane said to himself, pensively grinding his teeth, 'here you are, at the end of the world in a house that does not stand straight.'

He had confirmation of that at the end of spring, one day when he was on night duty. The whole peninsula used to come and drink at the bar of the Orebost hotel: farmers, fishermen, tourists. From May onwards a girl from the tourist office would play the bagpipes along the jetty, under the windows of the bar. The men working in the bar would bring her out glasses of beer and tips from the drinkers: they were delighted, absolutely enchanted, they used to assure her. She was a pretty girl who played rather well. Crane sometimes felt his heart throb for her. At ten o'clock she used to go home on a bike, and the radio resumed its sway. That evening the three last revellers—they were Dutch—went off to the sound of 'London Calling'. Crane locked the door behind them and they climbed to their rooms on unsteady feet. He turned down the radio, put straight the chairs, ran a broom under the counter, piled glasses, cups and saucers into the dish-washer. The dark waves lapped below the hotel, still darker now that he had extinguished the light in the bar.

Before leaving he ate a banana and drank a small bottle of Smirnoff Ice which he had set aside from the stock in the bar. The sky was overcast, the stars shining dim through the cloud. An aeroplane, a military aircraft, Crane thought, passed slowly over the coast at a height of several hundred feet. What was it carrying? Men, munitions, tanks? Crane had no idea. As a boy he had for some months entertained dreams of particularly exciting military adventures, dreams connected, probably, with his reading at the time. Later, his parents had offered a bicycle with a mini-motor in order to deflect him from a career which in their eyes was criminal and dangerous. He was thirteen, and he wanted, he told them, to become a fighter pilot; or perhaps a submariner. Any regrets, Crane? No. Following the aircraft with his eyes, seeing it dive into a bank of cloud over the sea off Orebost, he congratulated himself on having taken the long, twisting road to the Peninsula.

The aeroplane reappeared, winking its lights, huge, closer than he had at first estimated to the ground. An about turn in the clouds? A forced landing on the sea? Then, before his eyes it plunged into the sea, so swiftly that in the instant that followed he already doubted if he had really seen it. In the sea, not a trace. But what traces, after all, should he look for? Dismembered bodies? Yellow life jackets floating on the dark sea, on the black tide? He went down to the beach, watchful, circumspect. Some ducks were sleeping there, their heads under their wings. At the water's edge he looked back towards the village. Nothing there had stirred.

'So, Crane, you've been dreaming.'

ଓ

It took him a good half hour to get back to the bungalow. He arrived there worn out, his flesh goose-pimpled from the warm wind that blew towards him from the west. He stood his motorcycle near the wall, sat for a moment on the seat, and found himself so worn out that he doubted if he could manage to cover the few yards that separated him from his destination: the bed, clean and white, flanked by a few packing cases that served him in place of furniture. He could not bring himself to raise his eye towards the sky, the clarity of which, he sensed with bitterness, had been restored. He slept in his clothes in the tiny porch of the bungalow, not taking off even his shoes.

The following morning he watched the news on the three channels he received. During the night the aeroplane, whose fall he had seen over and over again, had acquired such a material existence that in the end Crane decided that the silence of the news-readers was concealing an embarrassing truth. During the day a more pleasant idea occurred to him. 'It is a failure of chronology, a weakness in the fabric of the universe. At sea off Orebost times are confused.'

Before going to open the bar he descended again to the beach, took off his trainers and turned up the ends of his trousers. Feet in the water, he looked out to sea. It seemed to him that in the course of the night it had become paler and less dense.

'If I went swimming there, if I drowned, what if I found myself in the war years?'

A childish thought, but it returned several times during the day to give him a delectable vision between the pulling of two pints of beer.

And the secret happening he had witnessed, the accident buried by the authorities? Crane talked of it in veiled words to one of the habitués of the pub, a retired teacher who kept a Bed and Breakfast on the road out of Orebost. The teacher—it was useless, Crane thought, to speak to him of contortions in time—gave him a lecture on the nuclear installations out at sea off the archipelago.

'That's a dozen miles or so away as the crow flies. Sooner or later, Crane, they'll prove their worth.'

'For what, Mr Gunderson? To launch against what enemy?'

They were joined by a crazy preacher from the Church of the Last Days, a Canadian with big blue eyes who had taken a room at the Orebost hotel for a month with the aim of evangelising the farmers of the Peninsula. Elder Doyle was of the opinion that the forces of Jesus Christ would eventually carry the day: meanwhile it was very possible that the armies of the Devil had by one means or another obtained an interval to sow destruction.

Crane, having regained his ramshackle hovel of corrugated iron and plastic, recalled the conversation as he went down to the lighthouse. The house attached to it was occupied. In the evening, light shone from the windows and there was linen on clothes-lines to dry, underclothes pertaining to both sexes and a red shirt the colour of a sail or of old wine: they flapped ceaselessly in the wind. It never entered Crane's head to envy these fortunate tenants. He took the little path that ran down to the Kilt, a tongue of rock folded by a freak of geology, the word for which Crane was too idle to recall. On the Kilt he and others over the years had erected cairns of many shapes, built out of fragments of rock that could be detached without too much effort from the more exposed blocks.

Crane went to sleep at the foot of a grassy slope after constructing two little stone towers at the far end of the Kilt. They wouldn't last. He woke at dusk. The wind had fallen, the air of the May evening had become suddenly soft. There was no more trace of his dreams than of the wreck of the aeroplane. Two skuas perched on a square rock flew off when he opened his eyes. The windows of the house by the lighthouse were lit up. Crane pulled himself together. He had a pain in the back. In his mouth was a taste of raw meat, which he explained in an instant. He had had a nose-bleed in his sleep. The blood had flowed out over his lips, his chin and his throat, and on the flat stone he had used as a pillow it had formed a pool, the surface of which was beginning to dry. He touched it with the tip of his forefinger. The skin of blood detached itself, tracing on the stone a spidery pattern that in shame he covered up with soil.

Above him towards the house people were speaking. Crane saw two red points glow in the twilight, and over the smells of the sea and his blood there floated the reassuring odour of cigarettes. He re-seated himself on the edge of the stone and waited for silence to resume. Before coming to the peninsula he had lived a year and a half in the Orkneys as a general labourer on a farm on Hoy. One Sunday, under the persistent gaze of a long-eared owl that had followed him part of the way, he had found on the mountainside the wreckage of a small aeroplane: grey wings lying in the heather, fuselage gutted. Crane had passed on his way without venturing to lean up against the windscreen. The aeroplane would doubtless rust away under the stars, the owl nesting in the fleshless skull of a hypothetical pilot.

'I should have gone back,' Crane thought.

ॐ

Towards one in the morning a large cumulus cloud, whitish in the night, reared itself above the sea. It held in it several gleams of day—something at that time of the year never far distant. Crane stopped thinking and absently scratched at the dried drops of blood on the sleeve of his coat. A little later, under the band of still clear sky that separated the sea from the colossal cumulus cloud, there rose a storm-cloud, thick and translucent, resembling the moving skirt of a gigantic jelly-fish. It trembled for an instant between sea and sky to give birth almost instantly to a dark red column veined with bright flames. Paralysed, Crane saw it pierce into the cumulus, merge itself temporarily with it and then slowly explode in an absolute silence proportionate to the distance. The cloud embraced it, swelled in its turn, expanded and was on the point, surely, of swallowing up the world. The stars, faint stars of the solstice, had been sucked into it. By the light of the monster Crane saw his hands trembling.

Slowly darkness returned; with it the murmuring of the surf. Crane was seated with his hands folded on his stomach, his head hanging heavy. At last he turned his head towards the house by the lighthouse: there, all was sleep. He returned to the bungalow not by the path under the lighthouse, which was too steep, but by the open moor, waking several sheep as he passed. Before going to bed he looked at the sea through binoculars. Of the gigantic jelly-fish there was no vestige. Crane went to bed not wishing to abandon himself any further to these dangerous observations. He slept for two hours, awoke at the first sound of bird-song. Or rather—was there some other noise? His limbs were still heavy. He went as far as the window of his kitchen-bedroom-sitting room, which overlooked the lake: it lay green and serene, reflecting the delicate morning sky. He opened the window, climbed on a box containing tins of food, and craned his neck to see flying high in the sky towards the east fighters in formations of three, so many of them that the spectacle lasted for more than five minutes.

The forces of Christ, was that it?

Still perched on his box he turned, an imbecile smile on his lips, towards the interior of the bungalow: towards the blanket of duck-egg blue on his bed, the racks of transparent plastic on which he arranged his small wardrobe and his crockery, the piles of magazines, covering music, fishing and body-building, the television, which he had been unable to stop himself from switching on at this hour of the morning—though it was now showing only programmes about animals, anacondas strangling unsuspecting jaguars, elephant cows giving birth, venomous Amazonian frogs.

'The forces of Christ,' he repeated, turning back to the sky where the last aeroplanes were passing with a whistling sound that was now audible.

ᘉ

That day he was on morning duty. What was he to do, however, in the sleepless hours that still separated him from returning to work? He turned off the television, treated himself to a lengthy hot shower, and a prolonged study of all the imperfections, the pustules, scars, blood-blisters and beauty spots with which his body was marked. Besides his nose-bleeds he had acquired on the inner side of his right thigh an abrasion he could not easily explain. It was the length of a hand, blackish red in colour, and it seemed already to have formed a scab. When he touched it with a hesitant finger it opened and blood poured out mixed, apparently, with pus. He had a brief qualm of nausea.

'What am I to do about a mess like this?'

In his medicine box he found something with which to disinfect the wound and cover its ugly mouth. After a moment the pain disappeared. He dressed and went off to work.

The bar was full continuously. At Fort James, seven miles from Orebost, there was a sports festival, a distraction much valued by tourists who doubtless liked to see men in kilts throwing tree trunks and emitting Pictish cries. Crane had hidden away the events of the night in a corner of his mind; he had not even looked for any confirmation. From time to time he felt his face give birth to a smile of triumph. Going to the lavatories he established almost with joy that his wound was sweating beneath its dressing, and that in his groin he had a haematoma, bluish and painful. He waited, however, till he had returned to the bungalow, his mind clearer than it had been for years, before he tore off the plaster and gauze to measure the progress of his malady.

He awaited nightfall with such impatience that, once the dressing had been replaced—he fancied, proud and resigned, that he had seen the bone glinting at the bottom of the wound—he swallowed two sleeping pills and slept for at least four hours. The night was not altogether dark. He got up, remade his bed, thought for a moment of going down to the telephone kiosk at Tullamus, from which he could have telephoned his friend in Glasgow and told him, perhaps, what he had seen and what he was going to see. In Glasgow, perhaps people knew—more than he? He changed his mind before he had even finished lacing his shoes.

He switched on the television and helped himself to a whisky with ice-cubes, to which he imparted tints from the screen as he watched, without really seeing them, two young women giving a lesson in Indian cookery. Just above the door a square fanlight showed the height of the mountain which overhung the lake. The blue-black of the mountain was traversed by a slow beam of light. A car? There was no road suitable for cars that high. A kid on a mountain-bike? Crane set forth just after midnight. In a small knapsack he carried a bottle of whisky, a pair of binoculars, an electric torch and his blue blanket. He went up to the path to the lighthouse. Some lambs with yellow rumps bleated.

The lighthouse or the cliff? The cliff had the preference. From the top you had a better view of the enemy forces. At the lighthouse, despite the late hour, he feared meeting Katie or her tenants, come out to look at the stars and smoke. He would have to speak to them, and he, Crane, had no more to say. Better still, he should go down to the lake with his painful thighs and unseen, take account of how he had lost that inner voice which, though prone to digressions, had nevertheless kept him company since childhood.

On the other side of the lake the slope was rugged. He slipped into a hole full of water and struggled out wet to the knees. If it had been full daylight and bright sun he would have undressed and coated his face and torso in mud; the night was cool, and he had no more room in his soul for these childish games.

Having reached the top of the cliff he squatted down facing the sea, the blanket over his shoulders. His heart beat in short pulses. On the path taken by the blood countless minute needles picked away at the partitions of his blood vessels. He waited. The sea was black, sluggish beneath a sky of a colour he could not define. Which was it? Blue? green? greyish? Concepts, these, that had now left him. Empty, yes, empty sky, non-sky from where were now falling in downpours those same needles that were shredding his veins. He shed tears of impatience; he told himself—who knows?—that those tears which were running down to his lips, and which in his exhaustion he was swallowing, were tears of blood.

At last they came, yes, in their hundreds, just before the rising of the sun. The sky was once more overcast and he heard them before he saw them. Their bellies stuck out below the clouds. Crane saw them open their fertile trapdoors. He had just time to cast off his blanket, and to lie down, arms crossed, eyes, mouth, thighs streaming blood, in order to welcome with joy his own private end of the world.

# PAN'S CHILDREN
*for Stepan Ueding*


ON the right bank of the Thay a path that was formerly used more by pilgrims than by shepherds crosses fields which in spring are covered with bluebells and wild garlic, and then enters undergrowth that harbours wild beasts I have no desire to see again.

I took this path one morning. It was late, because the fields of lucerne were burning, and the fires had escaped out of the farmers' control. The sky was stained with black, and for an hour or two I had worked in a chain of buckets that were filled from a branch of the Thay while we waited for the fire brigade.

The banks of the Thay, whatever the time of year, are more deeply peaceful than anywhere I know. A quarter of an hour's walk from the village there rises a church we call 'the old church' to distinguish it from the one at Murton. In its grave-yard are buried my parents and grandparents, and I too shall lie there one day, which I hope—or I hoped until recently—is still far off. The church is small. A storm destroyed its original tower, but the new one has now been standing for more than two hundred years. I stopped there, as I always do, and I saw through the gap under the trees that the blaze still continued. But at the old church one is already a long way from the world. Mass there has become rare; in the village and round about people prefer the church in the Main Street where we have an organ and a children's choir. I weeded round the family graves and pulled up the nettles, leaving only flowers.

Beyond the graveyard the path enters the forest. In time gone by, I reflected, pilgrims used to follow it all the way to the sea, some of them out of contrition or thirst for knowledge, and others, I am told, from a taste for roving. The journey to the sea took about ten days. In those days people travelled from church to church, and I used to enjoy imagining the evenings the pilgrims spent beside the Thay; in late spring to the smell of garlic, then that of honeysuckle, in summer hay, and lastly dead leaves and the earth under the bare trees.

That day I walked the length of the footpath which under the woods passes between the two hills of the Thay that the villagers of Murton call 'the Greater' and 'the Lesser'. The Greater has twin tops like paps; the Lesser has more height, but is pointed. The summits are bare, but the saddle which separates them is wooded with beech. As I crossed it I could hear lambs and, in the distance, dogs, but nothing from the village.

It was in coming down from the saddle, and still in solitude, that I heard other cries: a fox, I thought, but with more menace than its bark ordinarily holds. The path drops steeply to the Thay; below the hills, the valley is almost a gorge. There are very few anglers to be met with there; today I believe that the animals and other things which live in that part of the valley make the fishing bad. They eat the fish, or possibly the water is unhealthy, the water and the plants on the banks; or again the cries of the animals unnerve the fish and possibly the fishermen.

You descend right down to the bank of the Thay by a path that is abrupt and narrow, its edge reinforced by boulders and planks. In the steepest parts of the descent the walker can avail himself of ropes knotted to the trunks of trees. The beeches, the birches, the bluebells and the flowers of wild garlic make the forest more blue than green.

On this day, the day when three fields at Murton were on fire, I saw quite a large beast cross in front of me. Its coat was dark, it was less thickset than a wild boar and its snout was very sharply pointed. Sometimes the birds sang and made the branches rustle; at other moments I could no longer hear them, nor the river, nor the wind: only my steps, the beat of my heart, and certain other dull sounds that seemed to come from the twin hills, the Greater and the Lesser. Then, two or three hundred paces beyond where the animal had crossed, I saw the pale earth on the path in motion. Bending forward—the brown still river was glittering through the trees—I saw lying beside the path a living thing, about as long as my hand, twisting in the dust and puling like a child. The thing was formed like a child in other respects. It had two tiny legs and two arms, and two weak fists with delicate fingers, and a little round head with a crinkled face from which came a horrible mewing. Covering all its body was a kind of quilt coloured beige by the dust.

Going down on my knees and touching it with a branch I must have hurt it, for it wailed louder, and its body was seized by a violent trembling. I felt a temptation to touch it again to hear its cry, and also to crush its head with my walking boot.

I was on my knees. Several times I touched the terrible child with my little stick, and each time it twisted and opened its mouth and whimpered, but each time more weakly. And so, and because the idea of obliterating it would not leave me but was forcing black blood towards my heart, I cut through the woods to go down to the river itself without looking back at the infant, the infant-like creature.

But what sort of infant is no bigger than a hand and yet alive, fully formed and breathing? What sort of infant is cast like this beside a path? On the far side of the Thay the bank is flat and forms a meadow, which at that season is full of flowers. At the water's edge were growing irises and those big kingcups that lure our sons and daughters to drowning because they imagine them to be gold buttons. But I ought to have taken the creature in my hands and given it succour. I should have done that, I tell myself, if it had been a bird or a little dog. Or at least covered it up, hidden it, hidden its poor little death. When I was a child it was common to bring such little animals into the kitchen. Then you made a box which you lined with cotton; you fed them with a tiny spoon or a syringe. They died, most often, and you buried them at the bottom of the garden.

On the other side of the Thay there appeared the black animal, large and thin, that had crossed my path. It approached along the water-edge among the kingcups and took a long drink; then, something in the manner of a wolf, though wolf it certainly was not, it went down into the river and, having reached its preferred element, not without some effort, it allowed itself to float away, out of my sight and in silence.

I climbed back up the path. The infant had turned over, and I saw that its back was bleeding from many small wounds and scratches. The blood was already black and the flesh round the wounds was swollen and red. I unfolded a handkerchief which I had in my pocket. To this day I cannot describe the sensation I experienced when my hand, even through the fabric of the handkerchief, perceived the trembling of this miniscule body. Then the infant wailed and kept wailing, its eyes invisible behind their thick lids; and taking it up in my hands I saw the faint marks it had left in the dust.

A moment later it occurred to me to fold in the four corners of the handkerchief and knot them so as to carry the infant like a bundle. The blood stained my handkerchief. It seemed to me, when I reached the side of the Thay—a good mile downstream from the meadow where I had seen the prowling animal, though I kept a nervous lookout for it none the less—that the infant had grown heavier and perhaps larger. It emitted a thin, piping sound that never ceased.

They say that huge sheatfish live in the Thay. In the past I have seen snakes come out of it, and black insects with broad flat feet. That day there were also ragworms, fat and reddish.

Towards the south the river is more clear and forms big pools where our children used to go and swim. The infant writhed and wailed in its little bundle; I was afraid to look at it in case I should see its eyes. It was in one of these pools that, having removed my shoes, I drowned it, hoping thereby soon to lose the memory of how it looked.

That hope was vain. I let four or five big rocks fall into the pool on top of the tiny drowned infant, which perhaps might have lived if I had carried it back to my house in the village and fed it, without telling anyone; so that one night I might bear it back into the forest: 'Go, child of the woods, find your family.' And they would have come out of the forest—that family to which it belonged.

Then I went home by another path. In those woods the big bumble-bees fly so close to the ground that when it is sunny the dust and dry leaves stir under them. For a long time I watched them, or looked at the sun shining between the trees and on the leaves and through the delicate wings of insects—then took out my handkerchief—'The river—back to the river—it's the infant's winding-sheet.'

My throat was dry. I wanted to speak aloud; perhaps I should have been heard. 'Don't condemn me. That poor thing, could it have lived?' I pinched my arm, sat down once more not far from the river. The wild beast, I thought, was surfacing there from time to time; often I seemed to see its dark head in the water. At another moment I wanted to go into the river myself. But when I had put in my foot I thought of the infant and gave up the idea of bathing. I even fell to my knees again on the path. But what use was that?

It was soon dusk. I had not left the forest; I was lost. The paths always led me back to the Thay; but more than once I fancied I was passing the corner of the wood where I had found the infant. As for the tall dark animal, the beast with lean flanks, it often rubbed its wet body up against me and once or twice tried to force its grunting muzzle between my thighs. And others, too, of its kind, with thin spotted limbs, but brisker in their running: I did not know them, I could not escape them, for they were swift, they came silently in the night, nudging me without biting. Several times I imagined I could hear the moaning of the child—and I hung my head—and I fell. But most of the time I walked or ran down the muddy path—through the night—through the rain that came at its blackest hour—even through my sleep, the worst of my persecutors. Morning found me on a slope at the foot of the graveyard wall. My clothes were sodden, crushed leaves were sticking to them and to my hair. There was blood on my face; fear in the night, I think, had given me a nose-bleed.

In the evening after a day passed in sleep I saw that there were long cuts also on my arms and legs, of which some, the deepest, had bled abundantly. A little later I left that country, the Murton that I so loved, its valley, its hills, the Greater and the Lesser, and went to die, murderer that I am, far from the river.

# BRUNEL'S INVENTION

THERE were five of them going up to La Redotière, and already three of them were dragging their feet—they were hot, thirsty and now at midday they had had enough of this stony uphill road without shade. The man they met at the beginning of the forest path was coming down the mountain, a canvas hat pulled over his eyes. Brunel and Muscat dived under the beeches, but Secretan and Fleming squatted down on the roadside and brought out their water-bottle, while Sausserau accosted the man, contrary to the rules.

'Excuse me, do you know if it's still a long way to the sheep-fold?'

The man stared at the boys from under the peak of his white hat.

'Properly speaking, a good half hour: more if you go by the forest. Are you all alone?'

'Yes,' replied Sausserau, soon to regret it.

'But you're just kids. Aren't you afraid?'

Fleming stood up, feeling a shiver under his shirt.

'Someone's coming. They'll find us.'

'They'll find us,' echoed Sausserau.

In fact that was the object of the walk. They had started before sunrise from the campground at Les Alezards, one party making for La Redotière and another, led by Sauffert, the oldest of them and the one with real responsibility for them, for Maubranches. The adults had searched their knapsacks and

95

confiscated their mobiles. Secretan, indeed, and Muscat, did not possess them. They had to find La Redotière by map and compass alone. From the camp-site to St Alban's the way was easy and cool; after the chapel they climbed in direct sun, and the glare from the gravel of the path hurt their eyes. The sky, however, was far from blue. Clouds were swelling up in the distance behind ranges of hills of greater or less distinctness. Towards midday they heard thunder; then the clouds dispersed and the heat redoubled, even though it was not yet summer.

After the encounter with the man, the laggards cut through the wood to overtake Muscat, but without success. Muscat was the fastest of them, and Brunel always followed at his heels, afraid of being alone.

'Muscat is a real swine. He could have waited for us.'

'We could be dying, he wouldn't notice. Now he'll spend the evening making fun of us.'

'Yes.'

ख

The forest was of beeches planted far apart, where formerly medlars had been introduced. One was growing right up against a scrawny beech, and their trunks were intertwined, something that made the boys laugh. Secretan groaned. He had emptied his water-bottle to the last drop. In one of their rare silences (they chattered constantly) they heard a car pass on the road below. That couldn't be Josselin, one of the three adults in the camp: it was too early. 'You will spend the night all alone up there, but I'll come round about four o'clock to see you've got there all right.'

'Josselin! What a clown! He makes us walk for mile after mile, and as for him, he swans up in a car.'

'He'll have to walk a bit, all the same. You can't get anything to the sheepfold by car.'

'What? But he won't end up dying of thirst like me.'

'Is it true that he's going to bring loads of water to us?'

☙

Despite their secret hopes, they were not lost. At about three o'clock they reached the edge of the wood. From there a grassy slope mounted straight towards the great fold of La Redotière. Muscat and Brunel were waiting for them, stretched under a dead tree and letting their legs soak up the sun. Muscat was laughing. Brunel had taken off his shirt and placed over his stomach a sheep's jaw he had found in the grass. He was thinking of his father.

They dawdled up to the sheepfold, looking for flints, bits of bone, Roman coins. They ran baying after Secretan, who was considered fat. They made his nose bleed, and he pelted them with stones. Muscat, who was struck on the knee, bled in his turn, at which the others were envious. By four o'clock they were all bloodied in one way or another and shouting among the desolate mounds of La Redotière, their foreheads and cheeks covered with dried blood. Muscat told them to wash before Josselin arrived. 'He won't stay, anyhow. When he's gone we can get back to mucking about.'

Josselin arrived—they had heard his little car climbing up in the forest—and found them established in the shade behind the sheepfold. He inspected their knapsacks and judged the boys fit to pass the night alone on the mountain. 'Muscat, it's all right because you're there.' Muscat said nothing. He had blood under his finger-nails, and was sucking them as he listened to Josselin.

'You're in charge, O.K.? You're not going to play the giddy goat up there?'

A pleasure to which, none the less, they surrendered themselves as soon as his back was turned. They had climbed on La Redotière the previous year, in high summer, but they had been caught by a storm and not reached the crest.

ଓ

'There's a cave,' Secretan claimed.

'Where did you hear that, idiot?'

'It was Chauvin who was talking about it this morning.'

'Cave my arse!' said Muscat. 'Josselin wouldn't have left us alone here if there'd been a cave. He'd have been too afraid we'd go and look at it.'

ଓ

La Redotière was the shape of a pie sliced in half. From the shepherd's hut you ascended along the side of the hill without a path to the edge of the cliff. The highest point was called 'the Peak': the surveyors had marked it with a yellow board which also gave the altitude. From the Peak, on a clear day, you saw the whole range of the Alps. The boys, who were looking for the cave, hardly heeded it.

There was no cave, but a fissure more than a kilometre in length parallel to the cliff. At the bottom of the fissure the snow had not completely melted. A massive tree with bunched foliage grew at the southern end of the fissure. They carefully explored the side of the fault, and sounded the snow with a long stick without touching bottom. In places, however, the crack was more than two metres deep. Secretan suggested that they spend the night there, but the others shook their heads.

'It's going to be cold tonight.'

'We were dying of heat just now.'

'That was in the valley. We're up more than two thousand metres here.'

'One thousand, six hundred and twenty seven.'

The board on the Peak did in fact say 1627 metres. They walked along the edge of the crevice, their legs trembling under the influence of vertigo. Muscat walked close to the drop and leant over from time to time, still thinking of the cave. All along the crest strange flowers were growing. A short thick stem carried a single flower, blood red, the shape of a small bell. Fleming on an idle whim tore up some of these flowers and threw them on the grass. Muscat gave him a kick in the behind.

'You're a real thug, Flem. What's that supposed to do?'

Nothing, certainly, it was quite pointless. They gave up the idea of exploring the path which, once beyond the cliff, went down the other side of the pass into the beeches. The sun had set; when, precisely, they had not noticed. 'We'll doss down early, and go up again tomorrow morning,' said Muscat without much believing it.

They set off back in good spirits to the sheepfold, discussing what they were going to eat and drink. Josselin had thoughtfully brought up bottles of water, but forbidden them to light a fire. As they went, Muscat considered the best way of disobeying. What danger was there in making a fire in the sheepfold, under the open sky, between stones?

The first stars came out. Brunel, who was interested in them, went off to lie in the open and look at them. The four others argued about the right to keep up the fire and then to grill the sausages that had been already cooked and the slices of bread. An aeroplane passed overhead winking blue and red lights.

Brunel felt weariness attack him muscle by muscle. He raised his hands towards the sky which had become sombre: heavy stars, heavy Brunel, heavy earth.

ୡ

Fleming had burnt himself with a piece of bread. Secretan bound up his hand. Brunel, who had come back into the enclosure, suddenly fell asleep standing up. 'And on a ship, you know, you have to turn the handle for an hour to have electricity,' Sausserau was saying. Muscat yawned. 'What a life you had!' joked the clumsy Fleming with a laugh. Secretan had some cards. They grouped themselves round the dying fire and played by the light of an electric torch which Muscat had wedged between two stones. When the cold came down they went indoors.

Brunel saw dragons twirling beneath the bare roof of the shepherd's hut. Secretan was already asleep. Fleming and Sausserau were arguing about a minor point of play. 'Why wouldn't you let me play that? I'd have squeezed you. You'd have been helpless.' Muscat was reading in his sleeping bag, his back against the wall, his knees raised. A bird hooted at regular intervals—a scops owl, Brunel thought.

The light of the night was now leaking in, murky and faint, through the two low-set windows of the hut and the gaps in the roof. Fleming, who awoke for the first time towards one in the morning, heard the sound of steps outside, and shook Muscat, who was sleeping near him. The windows of the shepherd's hut were pale to the eye. The moon had risen. Muscat put his fingers on his lips, and Fleming, startled, opened his mouth. Muscat gently withdrew his legs from the sleeping bag, stood up, and went to the window, his back stooped. Through the window he saw the great slope of La Redotière swept by the wind under the moon. He made a sign to Fleming to get up and join him. They went out silently by the door beside which they had left their boots. Fleming shivered, more from cold than fear; but Muscat felt his heart, his intestines, sparkling with happiness beneath the mantle of his skin. They made the round of the sheepfold and, seeing nothing on the side towards the forest, took the path to the pass.

Brunel was sitting in a room with no light, holding a young swan with grey plumage on his knees. The bird collapsed, melted, dissolved on Brunel's lap; its little black eye, swimming above this disaster, still fixing the boy for a while.

'They've gone out.'

'What's that?

'They've gone out—Muscat and Flem.'

'You're joking.

'Just use your eyes.'

'They're mad.'

Brunel saw them in their turn file out, little Secretan and burly Sausserau; he heard without fully understanding their whispered exchanges, engulfed as he still was in his nightmares. He must have fallen back into sleep, wandering off again into lands of shadow, and was suddenly restored to wakefulness by a terrifying spasm. He found himself sitting up against the wall, his hands pressing on his stomach. He must have died in a dream. He didn't know of what. He held up his hand before the window, fingers spread, seething—with rage. 'The dirty swine, they've cleared off, all of them.' The square of light which the moon cast upon the cement floor of the hut was moving very slowly. Brunel got dressed. His stomach ached.

But walking beneath the moon under the vast sky of La Redotière dispelled the pain. Feeling some relief, Brunel went straight towards the pass and the cliff to which the others had surely preceded him. A small animal passed him running ahead in the grass: it was swift and long, a hare hardly darker than the herbage. The grass rustled. Brunel was at the foot of the steepest part of the slope, which led up to the fissure. He turned to look back at the valley. In the distance there were moving lights, motor vehicles, probably, on the mountain roads. A memory of the preceding year returned to him. He had been at the back of a car driven by his father. It was night. There was a medical broadcast on the radio. Brunel was looking at the clouds and the moon through the open top of the car.

ଔ

He found no trace, as he climbed the slope, of the big red flowers which none of them had been able to name. They had closed up; perhaps they had even sunk back into the earth. He bent over the grass, put his knees on a flat stone, and lifted his eyes. Towards the summit of the mountain, away from the moon, the sky was sprinkled with stars that you saw better, Brunel realised, if you looked at them with your head on one side. His anger came back to him.

The moon set before he reached the fissure. All the stars in the sky, he thought, had passed under his skin and threatened to transfix him. When he reached the edge of the fault, he first heard the air sigh and whistle; then he saw the night-birds, pallid and unresting, flying the length of the fissure and about his ears. His comrades, Muscat, Fleming, Sausserau and Secretan, were lying in the hollows of the rock with blood on their lips. The man in the white hat was trampling savagely on the four corpses. Brunel felt in himself a hideous rending.

ଔ

At La Sainte a lorry was blocking the road; a dog came barking in front of Josselin's car, soon followed by a young man with a sour face. 'Excuse me, I must get past,' said Josselin. 'I'm going up to the pass to look for my kids.'

'Ah,' said the man, 'We'll move aside in a minute. There's a queue. You must wait your turn.'

Two women were standing near the lorry. One held a lamb in her arms. Along the side of the fence, within a space of 100 metres, Josselin saw three heaps of dead sheep. Further on, however, lambs and ewes were going peacefully about their ovine business. Josselin, whose parents had a vineyard down in the valley, knew little about the diseases of sheep, and did not want to be held up. At the col of Veynes he took the bumpy track which climbed to the sheepfold where the boys had spent the night. 'I shan't go back by La Sainte. It wouldn't do to show them that.' He thought he saw other sheep among the beeches, alive, these, but cringing at the approach of the evil that had killed the others, or, worse, thought Josselin, of the vet's knife. In an epidemic, you slaughter the whole flock: that, at least, Josselin knew.

He stationed his car under the beeches; the rest of the way had to be made on foot, something that in the cool of the morning was not unpleasant. In his rucksack Josselin carried a thermos of chocolate and a bag of croissants.

He found the boys behind the sheepfold in the process of filling up a hole they had dug, they said, to bury a hare found dead in the grass. Secretan had eyelids still swollen with sleep; Fleming was yawning and cleaning his nails with the help of a carefully pointed match.

Josselin sniffed the air, pointed with his foot at branches turned to charcoal.

'Hey, boys, I told you not to make a fire.'

Muscat had already laid out at the foot of the wall, in full sunlight, Josselin's provisions. They squatted down and had breakfast.

'We were very careful, Josselin.'

While the others folded up their sleeping bags, Josselin took Muscat aside.

'You don't look as if you've had much sleep. Everything went all right, apart from the fire?'

Muscat had large brown eyes, in which the pupils, this bright morning, contracted to tiny holes. Josselin read nothing in them but tranquillity.

'Everything went super-right.'

'You didn't do anything silly?'

Muscat looked up at the pass and gave a slightly foolish laugh.

Josselin piled the kids' knapsacks into the boot of the car. They had competed for the front seat with vigorous kicks; Sausserau finally succeeded to it. The other three squeezed into the back seat. Fleming and Secretan fell asleep when the car regained the road, and Muscat, his stomach still slightly empty saw through the window the blazing stars of the past night.

# SHIOGE

YOU get to Shioge—when you need to get there, something seldom necessary—by a road that is well kept and almost straight: a little road that starts after the last house of Coll, makes a big circuit round the Peninsula, and rejoins the main road by passing through the Little Valley. Today, however, you turn back before the Little Valley, which is also called, or was once also called the Happy Valley; now the few houses that were there are falling into ruin. The roofs and walls are hollowed out by rain in the dark months; the summer heat bakes these wounds hard. All this dates, no doubt, from the year the sheep died, and the crofter of Shioge after them. The house in which he lived no longer exists, although from high up, if you know what you are looking for and where to find it, you can make out the site, and on certain sunny evenings the shadows of where its four walls used to stand are long and dark.

I do not know on what day it was that the sick lamb was noticed in the pasture that runs beside the road after the bend it makes to reach the Little Valley. Later a cairn was raised as a memorial of those bad times. At Shioge a sick lamb is everyone's affair. The lamb itself, standing in the short grass, was nodding its head unhappily, a strand of grass hanging absurdly from its lip. Its eyes were half shut, and it had on its back a wound as large as a hand, purulent and food for flies—and for other creatures, according to the crofter of Shioge, a man still young who had ceased, nevertheless, to look for a wife; not something, as he said, 'about which I much care'. This shepherd watched his lamb suffer for two days, and killed it on the third, in front of the other animals. It was too weak to be driven to the shed. On the third day it had sustained other wounds, one in its breast, another in the interior of its ear, and small ones about its eyes and mouth. The lamb was lying in a ditch, and trembled when the shepherd touched its forehead. The shepherd of Shioge killed it with a blow of a cudgel on its neck, and then threw the body into a pool of water on Nis—that is what they called the Peninsula that pushed its two prongs out into the sea beyond the village. There was nothing there but bog and dead heather. The man from Shioge, the shepherd, was afraid for his sheep and those of his neighbours, the disease being one to which he could not put a name.

'I should say it was a bird; an eagle perhaps, or rather a skua or a gull that's come to feed on them as they usually feed on carcasses,' the shepherd told himself; but he did not really believe it. These birds, he knew, never attack a living animal.

The following week he went to look over his sheep in the Valley and on the high ground. In good mild years like this he had a flock of more than three hundred, which he marked with a red circle and a green. Once he passed (without having intended it) the hole where he had thrown the body of the lamb. The water there was black. A soft warm rain came down and made Shioge think of lambing time, that peculiar time when the lambs, hardly able to walk, follow their dams fearlessly onto roads and into ditches. He loved such days.

At the end of the week he saw, high up in the valley, another sick animal. It was not one of his. The evil had bitten into the blue mark of Bua. When Shioge came back from above, where all the flock seemed healthy, he found a dead ewe. The same bird, he said to himself, had dug into its back with repeated stabs of its beak, though the thing was impossible. He did not remove the body; the wounds, he persuaded himself, were not the result of sickness. Nor did he say anything to the other shepherd, the crofter at Bua, since the bird's bite fell outside the realm of the possible, as did the nameless disease.

Nevertheless, two more of that year's lambs died at Shioge. By September the lambs were already large animals, but they succumbed in the same fashion as the first lamb and the one belonging to Bua. The deep wounds were to the back and the head, they knelt by the roadside and died, one finished off by himself, the other from its wounds. The shepherd climbed up to Bua but found no fresh animals taken there; the one he had seen before had been partly eaten by birds. That, said Shioge, is well within the natural order of things.

He stared at the carcass with some disquiet, and decided to spend the night in the sheep-walks. 'If there really is a bird that is attacking living animals, I shall surely see it eventually.'

The nights were still quite warm that year, and were preceded by red evening skies. The man from Shioge lit his pipe to drive off the midges that gather at dusk, and sat on the verge a couple of paces from the road. From there he could survey all the pastures at the bottom of the Little Valley and had a view of several lights: a pair up at Bua where two windows only looked over the valley, and on the other side in the distance (but the evening was clear) the green navigation light on the coast. From further still, there came a pale pulsation just above the horizon: it was the lighthouse of the other Ness, out at sea in the Atlantic. The shepherd passed the hours till nightfall watching these lights. Ordinarily he would go into Coll, supping sometimes with his sister, sometimes with a widowed cousin; he would return home by ten o'clock, switch on the radio, and fall asleep listening to it.

The apprehension which these destructive birds had been causing in him for several days kept him on the alert all that night. When would they appear? What would be their flight? Nothing came from the mountains; nothing came from the sea or from the further Ness; nothing rose up from the Valley. The animals were undisturbed. To keep himself warm, Shioge several times in the middle of the night walked up to the old sheepfolds from which it was possible to see some of the lights of Coll and the reflection of the Ness lighthouse on the water. On his first visit Shioge looked up and nearly forgot the purpose of his vigil: the stars were so numerous and so close.

Later he heard the barking of dogs: first those of Bua, the pair of them, then another he did not recognise, lastly his own, less fierce. The night was so clear beneath the stars that it was almost impossible to feel fear or anger. To Shioge it even seemed that the sea was being illuminated by a submarine moon. Seated on his verge he turned his straining eyes now on the water, now on the pastures and the peaceful sheep with their opal fleeces.

In spite of everything, after that calm night he found another injured lamb with the same wounds: its feet bitten, a frightful gash the length of its back. A chill came over the shepherd's heart, and he had not the spirit even to put an end to the animal's suffering. With the back of his hand he stroked its muzzle and forehead. Then he did a round of his flock; no other animal was affected.

At the end of the morning he climbed up to Bua. Wisps of fog were oozing out of the sides of the valley, ankle high. 'Perhaps that is what's killing my flock,' murmured Shioge, pointing down at the mist; but his mind was still on birds.

At Bua, the shepherd's wife offered him beer and shortbread. Himself, she said, was up in the hills. Shioge told her of his anxiety. Bua's wife nodded in sympathy. Bua and their elder daughter had found the dead lamb.

'I truly believe it's a bird,' said Shioge. 'Perhaps it's some kind of nightjar. They make hardly any noise. Or it might be an eagle of some kind we don't know.'

'It's something else, to judge from what we've seen,' said Bua's wife.

'A wolf,' said the other, 'if there are any still.'

'A wolf wouldn't let them live.'

'Well then, a fox.'

The woman of Bua shrugged her shoulders in a movement not without grace.

'If you like, Shioge, Bua will go down to lend you a hand,' she said. But in fact Bua did not come, and for the second night running the shepherd of Shioge gave up his sleep and experienced the uncertainties of the dark. The lights on the sea trembled, the dogs barked, probably between two and three o'clock, but the shepherd could not be sure, since he never had his watch on him. There also appeared in the sky, brighter than on the preceding night, a broad band of bluish or blue-green light. The shepherd, a man ignorant of history, thought he recalled things long forgotten, and in the hollow where he was sitting he smiled.

The following day, having seen nothing apart from the lights, and heard nothing except the dogs, the night birds, the sounds of his sheep and perhaps—but it came to him only later in the day, when he thought he heard a similar noise—perhaps the rustle of a small animal on the other side of the road—a lizard, if there were lizards at Shioge, or a blindworm—the following day he felt reassured. But before this noise came back to him he found once more, in a small field of his near the sea, two of that year's lambs tormented in that horrible lassitude which he could not now fail to recognise—there was no sickness like it.

In the afternoon he again did the round of his pastures. The dog, running between his legs or several yards ahead, was probably trying to find the scent of the enemy. Up on the hill ground he again found a dead ewe. The dog at certain spots on the way growled and tried to enlarge the entry to holes in the ground, either with its feet or its jaws.

The shepherd did not climb up to Bua, fearing, perhaps to make another discovery. The people of Bua were helpful but taciturn. He slept until nightfall to keep his mind fresh; perhaps he dreamed, I cannot say of what. A man like Shioge, of what could he dream? Of the night, of what came in the night, of what he could neither see nor arrest?

It was not a fine evening. It rained from ten o'clock until the small hours with a steady sound that was a harsh trial to Shioge's patience. Under cover of this constant din all the predators in the world might come to ravage his flock.

'The devil and his demons,' thought Shioge in the rain and the wind. He took a turn round his house, and went up the hill as far as Bua, where all was sunk in sleep. He stroked the blunt foreheads, woke up an animal that was sleeping on the road. The cloudy sky provided no distraction. Towards two o'clock he once more heard the dogs, and since their barking held more disquietude than on the previous night he realised that the dogs were scenting the passage of the enemy. From the road he tried to reconstruct its course. Bua had barked first, then Shioge, and then Shall, where the sound was deeper. After Shall there was a distant echo which Shioge could only just hear.

Shall was almost on the shore. The shepherd let out his dog and went down in the rain to Shall. His mind kept turning to things long past and absurd; he had the impression, for instance, as he passed the chapel of Shall, that he had gone into it one night as a small child and seen the moon through the stained glass; though this chapel was not one where he worshiped.

After Shall a track descends towards the sea. The Shall dog barked and Shioge's dog responded, but when they reached the sea it pricked up its ears and was silent.

Some sheep were sleeping in the shelter of the sand dunes. Shioge dared not inspect their necks or backs. Perhaps, he said to himself, they are all dead, so heavy, suddenly, was the air with universal death. At the base of the dunes—perhaps the people of Shall did not know of this bank of sand and this tree—at the base of the dunes a tree was growing just above a bank of grey sand. The branches of the tree were bare; the tree was dead. On each dead branch there hung what the shepherd at first took to be a small white bag; when he reached the foot of the tree he saw that these appendages were the skulls of sheep and lambs, the branches thrust through the holes for their eyes. All along the beach the dog ran to and fro, sniffing the bones under the sand, and the shepherd looked for a moment at the sea, which appeared to his eyes a crimson that was almost black. I think that among the mingled sounds of the waves and the falling rain he did not hear the return of what he had been following, the soft dark enemy.

☙

The following day the shepherd of Shioge, who had not slept, spoke to Bua about what he had seen on the beach and about the colour of the sea at the foot of that tree—a red, said Shioge, white-cheeked, so dark that he could no longer see his hand. At Bua, as usual, they nodded; but it was a part of the world they did not know.

'It's at Shall,' said Shioge. 'You must take the track to the left of the farm. The tree is not far from there, and its trunk is no bigger than this.' He showed his two fists held together. The man from Bua had found a sick ewe that morning. With her thumb his wife turned over the coffee cup, now empty, on the side of the table.

'There is no person like that, not here,' she said, at last.

'It is not a *person*,' replied the man from Shioge.

'Perhaps a bird,' muttered Bua himself, 'or it might also be a fox.'

'A soundless fox, maybe,' said Shioge, 'and black. Yes, a fox which the dog smelt, and which made it afraid.'

But his inner self said neither 'yes,' nor 'may be,' nor 'a fox'. He took his leave of the man of Bua and his wife without asking them to come down that night. His mind was now only upon his tenebrous adversary, that fox of the mist, the animal he must have missed at that grey beach, and upon the hunt for it, a hunt more or less heroic, with his dog leading, that would continue into the morning.

Shioge went to meet his fate the following night. Of the actual hunt there is no word; the unfortunate man never returned from it. I think that, as had become his custom, he had a sleep in the late afternoon, that he drank a glass of beer with his supper, and that he then went down to his lower pastures with his dog. During the day he had found two more ewes dead by the roadside. The beast had bitten them at the throat and again on the neck. Shioge kissed them on the forehead, his lips cold and bitter; and he dreamt, perhaps, of a brief and successful struggle, perhaps of the night in the chapel at Shall when the moon had shone through the sword of St George.

I believe that shortly after his supper he heard the rustling in the grass and the stealthy passage of the beast. I believe that his dog growled and hurled itself in pursuit. The shepherd followed behind it, and the beast led them both, dog and shepherd to the slopes above Shall, which break into precipices.

A daughter of the house at Shall, a child, found them dead in the morning, one of them half buried in the sand—the dog, already lacerated by gulls—and the other, the man, in a hollow among the rocks. Of the beast that was their enemy there was no trace; having vanquished it did not return. Shioge was buried, as were his dog and his maimed sheep. After which, sadness and night persisting at Shall, Shioge and Bua, men and animals eventually departed from what was still, despite everything, called the Little, the Happy Valley.

# III

# THE STORY OF MARGARET

# WHAT THE EYE REMEMBERS
*for Anne Guesdon*

## I

FANNY'S eyes were green, the muddy green of the bottom of a pond, and Margaret's were blue-grey, flecked with yellow round the pupils. Margaret and Fanny were childhood friends; they had shared the same nurse and various mischances. Fanny was the only daughter of a widower who kept an inn; Margaret was brought up by a well-to-do aunt and did not learn till she was thirteen of the tragic end of her parents: her mother had died of a broken heart when her father, an unmasked swindler on the run, went down with the *Belle d'Angers* on the way to New Orleans.

'Fanny,' asked Margaret one Sunday after Mass, 'how do you think a person can die of a broken heart?' Since their fate had been revealed, every night Margaret saw her mother in the throes of grief, and her father floating drowned in the Atlantic. The girls were playing pensively in the yard of the inn with Turk, a grey poodle.

Fanny made no reply. Margaret's lot seemed to her enviable. Why did not she have parents out of the pages of a novel, rather than M Boissonneau, bald and melancholy, and dead Mme Boissonneau, whose grave they visited every month? Buried with her were two little Boissonneaus who had made their appearance and departed long before Margaret was born.

'If only my father hadn't been shipwrecked,' Margaret asked, 'do you think he would have sent for us to America, once he was in luck again?'

'Perhaps he's not dead,' said little Fanny, rubbing Turk gently under his stomach. 'Perhaps he's living happily without you in New Orleans.'

'With a Negress,' said Margaret, drawing on all she knew of New Orleans. In her imagination Mr Cooper, her father, soon abandoned the black woman to die in her turn of a broken heart, and then came back to Europe.

That Sunday they were taking the dog for a walk beside the canal. They had already had lunch in the empty dining room of *The Canal Cross*, where Fanny's father had given them roast beef and beans. The smell lingered about their hair; Fanny, who was ashamed of this, was sombre, and Margaret silent. Near the lock on the way to Argenteuil they saw some men in a boat taking out a drowned man. A crowd of children were watching them. Margaret and Fanny sat on the bank and watched too, and Fanny caught herself wishing that the drowned man was her father, and that made her even more ashamed than the smell of burnt fat from the inn kitchen.

## II

Fanny was born on the 15th of April, and Margaret on the 13th of October, the one at Le Raincy, the other at Dieppe, at the hotel *Bon Retour*—if she had waited a few days more she would have seen the light of day in England. Both grew up in the home of Mme Bonnafé, a native of Grenoble who set up as a baby-farmer in Le Raincy. Bonnafé was a soldier and Mme Bonnafé was quite happy, she said, to have him away on duty. She looked after Margaret and Fanny till they were six. She was a large, fair woman and found consolation in gin, of which she drank a small glass every evening. She taught them sewing and embroidery.

Mme Bonnafé died a few days before Fanny's sixteenth birthday. One of her sons brought the news to *The Canal Cross*. His eyes were red and Fanny gave him a hug. Mme Bonnafé had 'had a stroke', he said; he was twenty years old, and had found his mother dead beside the fireplace. Fanny at the time was working in the café; she followed the boy back to the Bonnafé house where everyone was in tears. Mme Bonnafé was lying on her bed, her hands folded, a handkerchief over her face. Two Bonnafé girls were sitting at the bedside sobbing soundlessly.

Fanny remembered how one winter night she and Margaret had slept in this same bed alongside big Mme Bonnafé when the cold was biting. Mme Bonnafé in death had been put into her finest dress. Fanny could imagine the round thighs and the bulging calves of her nurse, and the great bosoms she had had. She felt a desire to lie close to Mme Bonnafé; she also wished, with all the force of her being, that the two little girls would go away—something they must have sensed. Left alone with the corpse, however, Fanny contented herself with raising the handkerchief.

Margaret and her aunt came to the burial of Mme Bonnafé. The aunt was still well off, and Margaret was not working: her aunt, thinking she had a voice, made her take courses in dancing, singing, the piano and English. After the Requiem, as they followed the hearse drawn by two black horses, Fanny spoke to Margaret of what she had seen beneath the handkerchief. Mme Bonnafé had died with her eyes open; it had been impossible to close them. Mme Bonnafé had looked at Fanny from the land of the dead. Margaret felt a clutch at her child's heart; she envied her friend. 'I would have spoken to her,' she said to herself, 'yes I would.' The open eyes of Mme Bonnafé seemed to lead straight to the limbo in which the souls of her parents were floating. 'I should have found the way.'

## III

Margaret became devout. Every day she went to Vespers at the church in Jourdain. It was after the death of Mme Bonnafé that she first saw, behind the priest at Sunday Mass, a huge eye open in the gilding at the end of the chancel. In the pupil of this eye ill-formed shapes were stirring. She did not speak of this either to her aunt, who was of a mocking temperament, or to her fellow students with Petit and Boismortier, who regarded her with curiosity because she was, they thought, English. Some days the eye did not open; but what unfolded in its depths was never the same. Even when Margaret found a place in the front pew, the forms in the eye were still obscure. One Sunday Margaret went to see Fanny at Le Raincy, but did not dare speak of the eye.

Her aunt had never encouraged these visits to Fanny, whom she thought common. The smell of the rooms in the inn now made Margaret shiver, as did the grease on the collars of Fanny's dresses. Beneath the stare of the gilt-lidded eye Margaret often prayed for her friend to be set free. When she went to Le Raincy the pair took the path by the canal and went past the fields to *La Gandinière*, a hotel frequented by the boatmen. These they observed from a distance. Margaret had no exact knowledge of men; Fanny kept company with the timid Bonnafé boy.

Fanny and Margaret were pretty, and sufficiently like each other to be taken for relations. Margaret was a little taller, with a higher colouring; there was nothing amiss with her except that her teeth were irregular. Fanny imitated her clothes and went every day to the public baths of Le Raincy, to the amazement of her father. When she was nineteen she left *The Canal Cross* and found work first on the Boulevard des Italiens as a shop-assistant at a mercer's, then in a glove-shop behind the Opera.

A chorus-master at the Opera removed Margaret's illusions, and she felt the better without them. She ceased seeing the eye, ceased attending Vespers, and read novels. All through the spring she thought she had discovered her father, saved from shipwreck and back in Paris, under the appearance of a bearded man with blue eyes who used to wait for her at the door of the Boismortier establishment, though without ever following her. He carried a cane with a silver top and, as a rule, a travelling coat. She showed him to Fanny, who considered him lugubrious. 'Why don't you go and speak to him?' Seeing himself an object of remark to Fanny, the man never came back.

Margaret dreamed one night that on returning to her aunt's house in the Rue de Rivoli she found this man in the drawing room, stooped over Fanny who was seated at the piano. Margaret went across to them and Fanny rose in tears, tears—she said, of joy.

'Margaret, Margaret, your father has returned from the dead.'

'I have died twice,' said the father, 'three times, many times. I died drowned in a shipwreck, I died thrown from a horse in New Orleans, I died of fever in the swamps of Florida. Ah, Margaret, the delights of death!'

At these words Margaret stretched out her hand to her father and looked into the depths of his eyes: 'This is the way.'


IV


Margaret and Fanny were once again like sisters. On Saturday evenings they went to the Bal Descottes, in the Boulevard Saint-Michel. Fanny lived frugally; the aunt, who was getting on in years, looked for a husband for Margaret. Descottes was not too disreputable; medical students went there, and young business men.

Margaret had a first adventure. One Saturday at the beginning of summer she danced with a student whom his friends called 'Père Lebleu', though his face was still that of a child. When the dance was over, Père Lebleu touched her hair with a look of ecstasy. They had both drunk deeply, and next morning she remembered nothing but a gleaming pavement and a strong light falling from a window; Père Lebleu took her in his arms and kissed her all round her eyes and lips. Fanny waited for them for two hours in a café that reminded her of *The Canal Cross*, and impatience made her shrewish. On the Descottes evenings Margaret always slept at Fanny's place.

They slept, as usual, in the same bed. Margaret in her drunkenness snored gently, and Fanny raised herself to look at her. She lit one of the lamps and put it on the bedside table. Without much thinking what she was doing, she sat down beside Margaret and with a trembling forefinger she raised one eyelid. The sleeping eye of Margaret looked at her vacantly. Fanny wept and bit her knuckles.

Père Lebleu did not last the summer. He was replaced by a dark, experienced boy who pinched Margaret at the base of her back and made her cry out. At the glove shop Fanny made the acquaintance of a frequent customer. Having first come to buy a man's gloves, he came back, he said on behalf of his sister. Cotton gloves, silk gloves, gloves of lambswool: he bought seven pairs in two weeks. He was not in his first youth; Fanny was surprised to find herself, soon, looking forward to his visits. This was not the feverish love of Margaret's friends, students with wet lips who drank to give themselves courage. Edmond waited for her one night when the shop shut. They went down to the bank of the Seine.

Edmond confessed his lie: he had no sister, only, he said, two brothers at Baccarat; 'But I found you very beautiful.'

'And what did you do with the gloves?' she asked smiling.

'I kept them for you,' he said, 'but perhaps you are tired of gloves. I made a parcel of them which I lost at the Gare de L'Est.' Edmond was pale-skinned, fair-haired with eyes that he often screwed up. His hand on Fanny's arm was light and friendly. At dinner she looked at him long and often without saying much. It seemed to her that all the dirt and bitterness her soul had absorbed since childhood was melting away in joy.

## V

Fanny went no more to Descottes. On Saturday evenings Edmond took her to a concert. Margaret shook her head and gave her friend a kiss. 'You remember Le Raincy? Remember Mme Bonnafé and the funny little dog at her house?'

'Don't be an idiot,' said Fanny. 'Were not going to be parted.'

The third of her students thought it would be fun to take Margaret to the morgue at La Salpêtrière. He showed her a woman who had died in childbirth and the baby she had brought into the world; the baby had a hole in its head. Margaret passed tremulous fingers over this half-head; in a spell of giddiness she saw, opening in the middle of the child's deformed forehead, an eye that looked at her. She put on a tight smile and in bravado asked to see a murder-victim. 'The pretty little ghoul', said the student, but all he could find in the drawers was an old pauper-woman knocked down by her husband.

Margaret too gave up the hectic evenings at Descottes. Her aunt had found her a young draper, a native, like the Coopers, of Bangor, whose father had sent him to Paris to sell their cashmeres and alpacas. Mr Cowie came to lunch every Sunday. They spoke English, Margaret sang songs and felt as if bayonet blades were growing in her belly.

Fanny saved Margaret from the attentions of Mr Cowie. One Sunday they went back to Le Raincy. Fanny's father had died the year before; *The Canal Cross* had been sold and then demolished. Fanny went arm in arm with Edmond; Margaret walked alone, her heart undecided. A cabriolet took them to *La Gandinière*, which had been smartened up and now offered music and dancing. A wooden platform had been constructed on the riverbank. 'We'll dance,' said Fanny.

A dark-skinned man with a roundish face came along, whom Edmond and Fanny knew. 'François! What a surprise!' Margaret was won over by this innocent device. M. François was shy, his eyes seemed restless. He danced with Fanny and then with Margaret. He spoke French with an accent that sounded almost foreign. He was Corsican. 'Both of us,' he told Margaret, 'are islanders.'

## VI

It was a double wedding. Edmond and M François were friends, just like Margaret and Fanny. On the wedding morning Margaret, dizzy with love, wished that her father might appear in all the splendour of her childhood recollections; but in fact there came from London only a bald cousin who could hardly speak a word of French. It had been necessary to assure him by a stream of telegrams that no one would ask him to pay the shipwrecked fugitive's debts. Her aunt and this cousin were the whole of Margaret's family; for Fanny there came the Boissonneaus of Chartres and Amiens. Edmond and M François were better provided with relations. The aunt found the Corsicans frightening. All the same, two old men who had come down from their mountains for the occasion made her dance like a devil-woman on the wedding night.

Edmond and M François, till lately a bachelor pair, used to share a flat above their workshop, a visit to which nearly caused the cancellation of one of the marriages. They manufactured glass eyes. 'Don't you see,' Fanny said to Margaret, 'that they're artists?' Fanny, after she was married, spent her days at the workshop. Margaret, whom her aunt had dowered generously, supervised the maid in the flat M François rented in the Rue des Acacias. The workshop was in the Rue Brey. In the window there was a huge plaster eye, the iris blue and yellow, which Margaret could never see without thinking of the death of her father. She went there rarely.

On the wedding night when Margaret and M François confronted each other in their new status, for some time they did not know what to do. M François was not a virgin; at Marseilles he had loved a dressmaker who was married to a customs officer. But these adventures were in the distant past. Margaret had had advice lavished upon her by her aunt and by Fanny. When she lay on her back to receive the bumbling homage of Mr François she imagined that at the tip of his member he had a golden eye with which to know her through and through. While he was at work on her she felt its gaze boring through her entrails. What did it see? A miniscule father and mother that she had kept warm inside her? M François did not seek them out; he marvelled at the supple waist of his young wife, at her small firm breasts, at a brown mole she had above her pubis.

## VII

Margaret and Fanny became pregnant the same autumn. At the workshop Fanny for a long time continued to keep the orders and accounts tidy and up to date. Margaret had no desire to know anything of the blind, the one-eyed and the mutilated who formed her husband's clientèle.

Margaret had many nightmares. At night when she was asleep her eyes would be stolen; they would be replaced by two glass marbles; and nobody but she would notice. But how, in this dream, could she see the cruel smile on Fanny's face, if she had no eyes? Another dream showed her the coming child being born without a head, like the poor monster she had seen in the morgue with Père Lebleu's friend. 'When M François takes me, he sees by his penis this headless child.'

Before they were too gravid they went back to lay flowers on the grave of Mme Bonnafé in the cemetery at Le Raincy. Margaret had never been able to speak to Fanny about this watchful eye. Fanny was in the midst of recollections. Corporal Bonnafé, back from military service, offered them coffee and cake. 'Mum would be really happy if she could see you so beautiful and well married.' The timid son had followed his father into the army. Two of the daughters were settled; the others worked in the garden. 'What was it called, that little dog Mme Bonnafé had when we were children?' Fanny asked. One of the girls replied it was Ulysses. Margaret and Fanny went off at sunset on a fine late autumn afternoon; the canal was frozen, boys were skating.

Fanny's son was born on January 3rd, Margaret's daughter just fifteen days later. They called the boy Pierre Emile Edmond, and the girl Marie Antoinette Françoise. They were both equally big and rosy, and so delighted the aunt that she bought them each, then and there, a silver rattle. She was godmother to both. Margaret did not get up out of bed immediately, and Fanny suckled both infants.

'Those bayonet thrusts that went into my belly,' Margaret said to herself, her mind away among the birds, 'they didn't destroy the child because she has come out of my body.' But later when she saw Fanny beside her bed holding the two infants, she imagined that they were both Fanny's and that she had lost her own. One afternoon she woke up under water. Her long hair floated towards the surface of the sea. Mr Cooper, naked, was sitting on a huge shell stretching out his arms for her. Sirens and Cyclopes danced around them.

## VIII

The August following, Edmond and M François left for Baccarat. Margaret's aunt and her maid took the two children to
Dieppe for the sea air; it was agreed that Margaret and Fanny
should join them when the ocularists returned. Margaret was in
low spirits. She came to sleep with Fanny as she had in the past,
at the Rue Brey over the workshop which had its blinds lowered.

'Fanny,' asked Margaret the second evening, 'do you believe
that they will come back? I dreamed last night that the train
went off the rails over a bridge.' Margaret had had no such
dream, but Fanny's calm industry was making her fret.

'Fanny,' she asked again, 'do you remember the man who
used to wait for me outside Boismortier's, whom I took for my
father? What did you say to him, that he never came back?'

Fanny was musing in front of a drawer of eyes that she had
brought up from the workshop and wanted to sort. Margaret
had let down her hair and was weeping softly, without Fanny's
hearing.

'Fanny, it was so dirty, so dirty and black, that odious inn of
your father's. Do you recall? When I was a child, my aunt didn't
like me to go there to see you, and nor did I, I didn't like it. Do
you remember?'

Fanny did not hear the rest—in fact she could not hear it; she
had gone down to the workshop, or else gone out to get help;
and Margaret sat before the fireplace in their room. The eyes,
which Fanny had left on the bed, looked at her with a hundred
glittering irises. One hand took her by the throat and squeezed it
for her gently; another wandered blindly over her face. Margaret was so surprised that she did not even think to cry out. 'It is
François,' she told herself, 'come back unexpectedly'. The hands
laid her on the bed.

The child was beneath the water, in the arms of Mr Cooper.
Two corals filled its eye-sockets. Margaret and Mr Cooper were

singing it songs of the sea-people. 'We have two children, and two eyes and two fathers, and two Margarets; the one is enthroned at Neptune's right hand, the other is in the Rue Brey at the window, waiting for her lover.'

'I shall pluck out one of your eyes,' said the hand, 'and make you swallow it.'

Margaret followed that eye that was descending into her. She saw again the wedding with M François and the clumsy night of nuptials. She saw again young Lebleu and his depraved friends, the nights at Descottes and the man she took for Mr Cooper; she saw again the handfuls of earth thrown on Mme Bonnafé's coffin, and under the beechwood lid her big open eyes; then the walks along the canal, and Fanny's thin neck, marked with grease under the ears, the fish they saw threading their way through the weeds of the canal, and the Bonnafé house, with its kitchen where there was always a wailing infant. At last the eye returned to the canal, and Margaret lay there, arms crossed. 'I shall not stir from here,' she said. 'This is where my father will find me, to take me to New Orleans.'

## IX

Margaret died on August 28th. A man working for the florist next door, worried by the stillness of the flat, finally summoned an inspector from the neighbouring police station. The policeman, Absan by name, had the door forced on September 2nd. Margaret was lying on the matrimonial bed, her face already fallen in. Her death was registered under the name Fanny by the florist's man, who did not know her well, and by Inspector Absan, who did not know her at all. As to the other Fanny—or the other Margaret—she had disappeared without trace, and the efforts made to find her by those who loved her were without success.

# THE HAND THAT SEES

### Mme Cholmondeley

MME CHOLMONDELEY is the most remarkable of my patients. A woman of great beauty, at the age of twenty-seven she was injured in her right eye by the oldest of her sons, then still a small child. The wound turned septic. The eye was lost; and by a cruel mischance the infection was transmitted—through the optic nerve, we think—to the left eye, which had to be removed too. Following very precise instructions from her husband, we made two artificial eyes according to the techniques of Messrs Boissonneau and Son, of whom in many ways I am the heir. These pieces of enamel reproduce with great accuracy the colour and shape of the eyes of Mme Cholmondeley, whose first name is Angela—Angela Cholmondeley, *née* Messer. The instructions, unfortunately, were given from memory and using as a model the eyes of the patient's oldest daughter, which the father guaranteed were almost identical with those of her mother.

The other day walking in the Tuileries with Margaret, I met Mme Cholmondeley accompanied by two children, one of whom, I think, was the involuntary cause of his mother's misfortune. M Cholmondeley was holding his wife's arm, and she as she walked was balancing in her free hand a white umbrella—or perhaps, I'm not sure, it was pale blue. M Cholmondeley, whom I don't pretend to know socially—such are the rules of us makers of artificial eyes—M Cholmondeley did not greet me either, though in the intimacy of the workshop he pays me the highest compliments on my workmanship. Margaret pulled me by the sleeve in her childlike way.

'That woman—' she said to me, '—did you see her? She was staring at you. What beautiful eyes she has.' To this I could not reply with what I knew of Mme C's fine stare.

Margaret cannot for a moment imagine what an eye-socket looks like when, by accident or disease, it has lost its eyeball. She knows my profession, of course, but in the innocence of her mind she does not picture its strange details. She is still a child, snatched by Mme Boissonneau junior from the claws of a depraved mother. Oh, I who know Margaret better than anyone, I am sure she would rather have died than follow the example of her mother who, wicked as she was, had given her at the outset some instinct of religion. Margaret is someone whose devotion passes understanding. We have in the bedroom a small altar before which she prays night and morning.

I do not know why, but the fixed regard of Mme C sent through my body, while we were in the park, a burning desire to find myself instantly in our bedroom, and to have before my eyes Margaret's lovely back, her neck bent, kneeling at prayer in her night dress. The idea of entering her at that moment when she is full of her God enchants me, and I often dwell upon it until the day when she tells me, in a voice not altogether her own, that I ought to put aside such thoughts. Has she caught my look, reflected, perhaps, in the silver-gilt cross that dominated the altar, and has she in her innocence read in it my thoughts?

I placed my hands on her shoulders. 'What is it, dearest Maggie, that I should put aside?'

Her face was wet with tears.

I might say that I am better acquainted with the body of Mme Cholmondeley, in whose injured sockets I have several times already, under the anxious gaze of her husband, inserted eyes I have made (I say 'several times' because these eyes become worn and need changing) than with that of my own wife, who does not allow me to approach her except in the dark, and to whom my caresses bring tears, though she says she loves me, and loves me with all her heart.

The first time she came to the Boissonneau establishment Mme C was wearing a brown silk dress and had on her head a straw bonnet to which was attached a thick veil that concealed the sad spectacle of her eyeless lids. To tell the whole story, Mme C fainted when we wanted to examine the eye sockets, and I saw her naked bust, her desperate husband having unfastened dress, bodice and undervest.

## Margaret

Margaret was thirteen when I met her, and I must confess that I have no other recollection but that of a child with a rosy face who said not a word but kept blinking her eyes so much that I thought her sick. Already devout, she went to church three times a day accompanied by Mme Boissonneau junior, the wife of my master, who had taken her under her protection. I often used to meet them, Mme Boissonneau nearly always wearing a veil with her hat, though she is a good looking woman, and Margaret with a bare head and a dreamy, almost mindless stare. Later— one or two years having passed, I don't recall—she spoke to me. It was in the gardens of the Champs-Elysées, and I saw that she was beautiful, to my eyes at least, and that I should have to share her with Our Lord Jesus. Margaret never comes to the workshop in the Rue Vivienne; unlike Mme Boissonneau junior, she is made to feel unwell by the work on the eyes. Mme Boissonneau, in contrast, does not disdain to help us when the need is felt. I did not see Margaret except at the Boissonneau house, and then had only the briefest glimpses. Not that Mme Boissonneau was a stern sort of woman; but she was afraid that in Margaret the vicious proclivities of her mother might one day manifest themselves. So for a long time Margaret ate with the children, and up to the age of eighteen she did not appear until after the liqueurs, when she would sing while one of my master's daughters accompanied her on the piano. She was of the same age, hardly younger, this other girl, but she might have been made of glass or mist, I never saw her. Margaret's singing was neither very loud nor very true; she had the slightly drawling and affected voice of her mother, whom I met after we became engaged. There was some reluctance to let me see her, this Mme Cooper, as she liked to be called. She lived in a mezzanine flat in the Rue de Bonne-Nouvelle, and described herself as being of independent means. She was a small woman with a round face and an ample bosom; she dressed in a quiet grey silk, and her only real attraction was a pair of very blue eyes, which Margaret did not inherit.

'They tell me that you are marrying the girl I gave for adoption to these manufacturers of eyes, and that you yourself are one of them?'

The walls of her sitting room were hung with paper the colour of blood; one crucifix hung over the mantelpiece, another between the windows which looked out onto a courtyard cluttered with old furniture.

'I shall not embarrass the girl you are marrying by coming to your wedding, Monsieur,' the Cooper woman continued. 'But come near so that I can look at you.' And she made me sit close to her and looked deeply into my eyes.

'You will do harm to her, Monsieur,' she said, placing on the centre of my forehead the index and middle fingers of her left hand.

I do not know what insight this woman had into souls. I did not go back to see her again before my marriage, even though an urge to do so came to me once or twice. As to her morals: I believe that despite the crucifixes and her advanced age she still lived on her charms.

Margaret, whom her mother had *given* to the Boissonneau family when she was only eight years old, tells me that her mother had come from Ireland accompanied by an American; he had died, according to my naive wife, before being able to marry Mme Cooper, and that was the cause of her fall.

'My mother will not go to heaven,' Margaret often says, and she prays whenever she can for the salvation of her soul.

*Yet Margaret carried on the inside of her thighs and under her left arm little round marks where her mother burned her as a punishment, using a spoon she had placed in the fire.*

'Punishing you for what, my poor innocent child?'

When I put this question, Margaret lowers her eyes and says with a blush that she doesn't remember. The love of Christ, she adds, has 'come back into her through these wounds.'


## My Childhood

I have sometimes had this thought, that I share with the Cooper woman a strange resemblance: that the two of us came from a very dark world and that it may well be that she and I both passed too quickly into the light. I should have preferred not to have any recollection of the mountains where I was born. They are black, and smell of dead flesh and burnt wood. It is possible that one of my earliest memories is that of the carcass of a ram, its belly torn open by crows and vultures, carrion birds which I and other children from the village drove away with stones. It is possible also that this memory is of a dream, for when I think back it seems to me that the vulture, when struck full on the head, stood up like a human being and disclosed under its great wings the breasts and round thighs of a woman. The sky above our mountains suddenly out of a burning blue caused little flames to flicker up on our lips; soon we were dead, at the feet of this female griffin. Another memory, more reliable, is that of my parents' house, a forge on the road to the abbey, and a sunny afternoon I spent playing with a puppy that one of my uncles had given to my brother Jean-Baptiste. Also a harvest procession, led by the priest who was followed by a cohort of children; the huge cross he was carrying flashed in the sky as though to cut it in pieces. Nevertheless I am never sure of my memory; what I think to have been the case is sometimes no more than an illusion. It is so with an evening I passed with my godfather at Bonifacio a few days before embarking for Marseilles and leaving my native country never to return. I walked until late in the day with him on the seashore, the eve of my departure. It was a Sunday. Armand Filippi, my godfather, who was also some sort of cousin of my mother, had obtained a place for me at the Lycée Thiers, at Marseilles, through his brother who was vice-principal there and with whom I lodged for two years before leaving for Paris, my baccalaureate in my pocket. I do not know how to describe the effect upon me, after the mountains and the sad years of my boarding at Ajaccio, of the blazing white beaches where my godfather that evening showed me the women fishing for eels, their legs and arms bared, pulling out of the sand the long fish which they threw living into baskets. Sand lilies were growing on the rocks all along the beach. Armand Filippi made one of the fishwives prepare two eels; she cut off their heads while they were alive, and sliced them up on a flat stone. We ate them cooked over a wood fire on the beach.

'Godson,' Armand Filippi asked me that evening, 'are you a virgin? What career have you in mind?'

I was indeed a virgin, and I imagined myself becoming a doctor.


### Mme Cholmondeley

Mme Cholmondeley came back to see us for her fourth refitting, according to our register of appointments, on July 17th, 18—. The previous evening Mme Boissonneau had informed me that

Margaret was pregnant—she herself was unwilling to speak to me *of such things*. At that time, influenced, no doubt, by her increasing devotion, I kept having a terrifying dream of a dead priest whose body, so swollen that its bones were bursting out of the skin, was putrefying on the beach, a fat jelly-fish draped in black. My godfather, Armand Filippi, identified this corpse as that of a parish priest whom he had killed, he confessed with tears, in order to *rob* him. I ought to say that M Filippi had died in 1879, leaving me a sum of money that enabled me to buy our home in the Rue Brey. This dream of the dead priest, as I called it, so troubled me that it almost spoilt the pleasure that I took in attending on Mme C with her enamel eyes. An unforeseen circumstance, however, soon made me forget the dead Filippi and his imagined crimes. Mme C, contrary to her usual custom, had come accompanied not by her husband but by a woman of ripe years, with a good simple face, who had become one of her devoted companions, reading aloud to her, no doubt, and taking her to concerts, to her dressmaker, and to Mass. But this woman did not stay in the workshop while I changed Mme C's eyes.

'I should rather, my dear, that you waited for me in comfort, and knew nothing of this piece of juggling,' Mme C asked her: kind Mme C.

But what can she really know of the effect on people of her perfect face when it is deprived of its eyes? What images of her beauty arise in the clouded darkness of her thought?

'My husband,' she says to me while I am preparing my instruments, 'has gone off to the Caribbean to inspect a property left to us by my uncle. What use is it, Monsieur? We already have so much.'

She did not say another word for the rest of the sitting. She breathed slowly, her nostrils flared, her hands joined on the stomach. What terrible, inexhaustible bliss, to be able to see this woman without being seen. And to slide under her eyelids the metal eyes in the enamel of which I am reflected, avid and miniscule, in the black depths of pupils that cannot move!

'It is done, Madam,' I tell her in expressionless tones, not daring to touch her for fear of betraying myself. I open the door and call in her patient friend. I have stored up in a box four pairs of eyes already used by Mme C: the secretions of her sockets, the tears of a year.

## My Dreams: The War

What am I to say? In Paris I was unable to become a doctor. For those studies you need an intelligence and an appetite for hard work with which I was not endowed, also a material support of which I was very swiftly deprived; M Filippi, my stern benefactor, saying he had no desire to encourage me in idleness. After two years in medical school I should have had to find a way of earning my bread; but the war with Prussia sent me down other paths. As a medical orderly all I saw of fighting was wounds, severed limbs, bellies slit open, men starving and sick whose plight left me in the end insensitive. Altogether, it is hunger that I recall most often (for I too experienced it) and the sight I had at Morsbronn of a naked man, his skin bright red, following the soldiers with his hands covering his ears. Still, it was at the war that I met my compatriot Alexander Borgo who, in 1872, got me to enter the firm of M Boissonneau; the same year my father died and my brother Jean-Baptiste joined me in Paris.

## Mme Cholmondeley

The memory of Mme C's visit causes in me fits of increasingly deep musing, to such a point that at certain moments in the day, particularly when I am at my work table, colouring an eye, a curtain of thick velvet descends, not on my outer senses—I can still see and hear—but on my soul, withdrawing it from the contemplation of what surrounds it. To tell the truth I have the feeling at these moments that, despite the distance which separates us in the ordinary way and which I cannot measure with exactitude, I am visiting the consciousness . . . no, the very mind of Mme C. I have only to lay down the paint-brush, close my eyes, and I hear another world. The sounds of the workshop are still there, but I am at the same time in the centre of Mme C, in her chest, in her bowels, I lodge myself there with an unspeakable joy, and I experience with her in the same bewildering shadows the manifestations of the world outside her, the deep grave voice of her husband, the happy ebullience of her children, their loving hands upon her cheek, her bosom, her stomach.

Margaret, of course, is completely unaware of these transports. Here I am, I think to myself, inside Mme C in the same way in which our child is inside Margaret, but with the difference that I can hear and understand what goes on around Mme C, and besides I am so happily at home in her that I should like never to go out. Whereas seeing Maggie so enlarged gives me horrible presentiments. Come the night, I see our little one floating limp on a tide of blood that pours from Maggie's gaping vagina. Or that the child is going to be born already old, shrunken and wrinkled. At other times I imagine that with his nails he is labouring in the dark to tear open the flesh that holds him prisoner, and that, once freed, he will strangle us and make off over the roofs. The times I spend in the workshop in painting, in burying myself in Mme C, draw me happily away from these imbecile fears.

M C has returned from the Antilles. At times it is his voice that I hear, without finding it very reassuring. His fingers grasp the wrists of the exquisite Mme C; and there are other movements, much more tender, which my fantasy makes me spy upon, at night, when the innocent and gravid Margaret is lying beside me. And why, Margaret, why will you not let me enter into *you*, why will you not allow me the place that you give your child and your God? *But what does it matter, after all, since here I am, whenever I wish, the intimate of Mme C?*

### Birth of the Infants Marie and Padoue

I was at the workshop, and my hands were working on eyes, though my spirit was bathing in Mme C, when Margaret was seized with the pangs of labour. A messenger brought me the news, and I stopped at the Café-de l'Arc before going back into our house, not that I was not eager to see my wife and our first born child in her arms, but, to be honest, I had an indescribable fear of the strange appearance the child was bound to have. At the café after my drink I had three visions of it: a little round creature with a gilt forehead, resembling a Chinese idol; an eel with a human face sliding through green water; a child already grown, dancing on its mother's stomach. The alcohol that had aroused these images gave me a certain courage. The nurselings that I was surprised to see beside my wife had nothing odd about them except that they were two in number. They were marvellously healthy; only their cries, loud and unceasing, tore me away from Mme C.

It often came about at that time that I slept at the workshop, where a bed was made up for me. Far from reproaching me for this distance, of the real cause of which she knew nothing, Margaret said to me, her eyes lowered, that she felt quite happy to sleep alone with her babies, her thoughts upon God.

### I Haunt Mme Cholmondeley

I enter Mme C at the place where I insert her enamel eyes; often I plunge from there into her oesophagus and feel my way down to her intestines beneath the satin of her stomach-muscles. Her husband, an ardent lover, places his hands there and pours out in a low voice amorous protestations that make my own entrails quiver.

## Funeral of Mme Cooper, my Wife's Mother

My mother-in-law dies of a stroke seven months after the arrival into the world of our children. It is in going to pay her a visit with one of the twins that Margaret and I find her unconscious under the window of her sitting room, which she had been opening or shutting, I don't know which, when her seizure occurred. Margaret sits on the ottoman there stunned; her tears flowing over the child she holds in her arms. Mme Cooper is not yet dead; her large eyes are open and fixed on the ceiling, and a rattle comes from her throat. Am I to leave the unhappy Margaret alone with her dying mother in order to go and look for a doctor? The Cooper woman is glad to stretch herself out in my arms while her distracted daughter prays for the salvation of her soul. Innocence, innocence!

'Her last breath', she tells me that evening 'floated out in the sitting room; don't you think my poor prayers have escorted her up to heaven?'

And I, clasping in my arms the remains of the sinful woman —O Margaret Cooper, ungodly mother of my beloved Margaret—loved, even if badly, even if betrayed in spirit day after day with the most ridiculous fantasies! There comes to me in the funeral Mass an ecstasy I had not anticipated. While an idiot of a priest who knows nothing of the old witch muddles through his sermon I dive for the first time in three days (the memory of Mme Cooper's burning gaze on the brink of death held me back all that while) into Mme C with even more abandon that usual. So much so that, when her child lays its head on its mother's breast, and murmurs to her with some story or other about a parrot that doesn't want to return to its cage, I have the feeling that I am the kind, shadowy soul of Mme C; the

137

hand that strokes the face of the weeping infant is mine. Note this, I ask you: I dissolve into Mme C without her having the least consciousness of this; I am an invisible guest who never speaks to her, never weighs her down. Do you know what it is to hear from beneath the skin a child's voice and that, apprehensive and serious, of her mother?

Margaret, kneeling in the pew, her veil drawn over her chin, is not weeping but pallid, praying for the impossible salvation of her mother. Mme Boissonneau, next to her, puts her arm round her neck. Margaret, I know, is once more filled with countless angels. I see them shining under the skin of her forehead and her cheeks. The same evening as she takes off one by one the simple garments that show her mourning, I see them again, distending her breasts and her belly. I thrust in to meet them, not with the joy I obtain from my union with the darkness in Mme C, but with pleasure all the same. I drown these tiny cherubim in my semen.

## More Reflections. The Eye

On my return from the war I learnt my trade for three years under M Boissonneau, I measured eyes, copied them, painted them in the finest detail to order—I am, I know, a skilful craftsman—I managed to make them good likenesses; better still, I made them *seem to see*. I was able, even though I am no *artist*, to find a means of giving the enamel a sparkle, a brightness, in short, an illusion of living flesh. If I place one of these eyes in the hollow of my palm you may see me filled with demonic joy. Many times I have imagined myself caressing Margaret and Mme C, both lying on the same double bed, with my hands so filled. I seem to remember that when I was a child in Corsica, we ate pigs' eyes cooked, and the first one-eyed man I saw was one whose eye had been torn out by an eagle owl. On battlefields I have seen many eyes blinded. When Margaret is asleep I sometimes put my mouth over one of her eyelids and breathe lightly in. I have no yearning to have within me an eye belonging to this poor child, to drown it in black bile and absinthe, no, it is I who would like to visit her with my roving globe, in the way in which I have for several months chosen to make my home within Mme C.

## Conception of the Child Antoinette

As soon as her mother has been buried my foolish Margaret is seized with pointless guilt, and refuses herself to me night after night. This causes me no suffering, sated as I am by my sojourns in Mme C. One Sunday, however, when with Margaret we go walking at Poissy and, hands folded over her stomach, she falls asleep under a tree, I have an urge to take her there and then. I am checked by the presence of Mme Boissonneau, detestably kind and maternal, who holds against her chest our child Padoue, now aged a year and two months: a double shield of flesh, I say to myself, guardians and protectors of my silly wife. She sleeps, eyes shut and mouth open.

And why am I so much at my ease in Mme C when I hear, evening and morning, the amorous compliments her husband lavishes upon her, when I feel the caresses of the husband who smoothly guides his wife's hand, and still more the stiff male member which works in Mme C, dry, rapid, and evoking joy, sighs, laughter? The body of my wife is opaque to my gaze. She undresses without any real awareness of my love. The evening following that walk, however, when I had desired my wife as she lay on the ground, bits of grass on her face, I wait till she is asleep and am careful not to immerse myself in Mme C. This is how I take Margaret. Blindfolding her once she is asleep, and making a gag out of one of my ties, I come into her with great violence; I teach the angel a lesson, so to speak. The pain wakes her; she would like to cry out, but she cannot. I draw back after having ejaculated, and bite my hands with shame, my hands that pretend they see, while she wails and tries to free herself from her bonds. She is unable to. She raises herself, she falls and stays on the floor, sobbing away. As for me, a felicitous black wave has already carried me to my home within Mme C. She is, I can tell, asleep; some day I shall see what she dreams.

## Benefits of Absinthe

One afternoon as I leave the workshop I see my wife coming out of a church in the Rue Vivienne together with a priest I do not know. She is again big with child, he is tall and thin, and yet the particular position of the sun in the sky gives them shortened shadows, dark and gleaming. Maggie is wearing a red dress which came to her, I think, from her mother. The priest has taken her arm and is speaking in her ear. I go to the café, for I find in absinthe a means of subsiding more rapidly into the intimate depths of Mme C, though this route makes me proceed by deceptive byways. Am I right to drink when at every moment there is accessible to me the strangest country in the world? *Once at the Demi-Coq, which is in the Rue de Courcelles, I thought I saw, projected on the cortex of Mme C's brain, images of her life before she went blind.*

Has my wife, I asked myself later, revealed to this Jesuit the brutalities I have inflicted upon her—and not just once, but six or seven times, for her feebleness fills me with rage? At last, one morning at breakfast, she takes a knife and slashes her palm without a tremor.

'Why are you doing that, my poor child?'

'I did not think,' she replied, strangely sarcastic, 'that you could feel any emotion at seeing me suffer.'

As a result of that I left her in peace. She is the most indecipherable person. She spends her days with our twins and goes to Vespers with Mme Boissonneau, whom she looks upon as her mother. Every evening she lays out the cards to tell her fortune, and she reads nothing but the Bible and edifying novels lent to her by her great friend. The maid told me one day that as soon as my back was turned she would sing.

## Our Vows Renewed

Some days after the birth of our Antoinette (oh, I know she is mine, in spite of the priests and a dream I have had twice of the Cooper woman sitting on the edge of our bed, her thighs spotted with blood, casting insolent glances at me: 'Wretch! She will be every man's prey') I have the agonising happiness to see Mme C again at the workshop, accompanied by a child of twelve or thirteen who must have been one of her daughters. *Without her knowing, I renew our vows.* Immediately afterwards I have to top-up with absinthe . . . yes . . . the joy that came over me on seeing her once more, perhaps for the last time, for, she told me, they are all leaving for the Antilles where her husband wants to develop his property. At my wife's bedside I must confess I have paid less attention to the confidences of Mme C's husband, taking refuge within her in order to sleep, if you will, and find tranquillity. Maggie does not recover quickly from this latest confinement. Our maid busies herself with the twins and Mme Boissonneau visits them frequently.

Here I am, lying on the sofa in our sitting room, as I muse about the coming of Mme C to our workshop, and am borne up by a yellow sea which she will be crossing in a few weeks on the way to a new world from which I shall be separated only by the thickness of her skin and muscle. Tropical birds, monkeys, snakes, I shall hear you as well as she does. Look at me, about to fly beneath the huge dome of her soul, now grown colossal. I do not know too well where she is or what she is thinking, yet I am able to make this reflection; that she is asleep and I am revelling in her dream. I am your microscopic lover, Angela; your sweet parasite, the calm eye in your depths.

## Crossing

It is the day that the Cholmondeleys embark for Fort de France, on a ship the name of which I do not know, though from the workshop, while examining the socket of a little girl who had lost her eye through a dog's biting off her cheek, I sense the bustle of their departure. M Boissonneau over lunch puts to me his proposal. His fortune being made he wishes, he says, to retire to the country and find for his daughters husbands that are not ocularists.

'In fifteen or twenty years, my friend, when your daughters are of an age to leave the nest, you will have the same desire.'

This news, which ought to have delighted me, is unwelcome and upsetting. Leaving the workshop late I find it necessary to go to the Demi-Coq to drink, or to drown myself, I don't know which, in several glasses of absinthe. The twins with their little legs are dancing on my head. Light as they are, while they are there I cannot enter into Mme C, a new and terrible situation. In my fancy I catch my children by their collars and throw them into the sea. Returning to the Rue Brey, I am so dazed by these unexpected developments that I pass in front of Number 11, where we live, without noticing: when I reach the end of the road I am amazed at not having found our door. I retrace my steps with my mind a blank as far as the Arc de Triomphe, at the time when the sun is setting, red and shimmering. In the end, I have to re-enter my gloomy dwelling. Margaret has still not risen from her bed; it is our German maid and sometimes Mme Boissonneau that take care of our children. I sleep in the sitting room; not only does my presence, I think, reawaken in Margaret a disgust which in her exhausted state she no longer troubles to conceal from me, but I feel that when I sleep beside her I breathe in the odour of her suffering all the way to my refuge. The door is black and tight shut, and the two children, their forms pale and thin, guard it against anyone who knocks.

'The way in,' they say, 'is closed.'

There remains one resource, a sombre one: the eyes of Mme C, which I hurl in their faces. I have them, you understand, kept safe in a box, those eyes that she wore, that she washed with her tears, eyes that were my sweet path into her.

'The way in,' they repeat, 'is closed.' Their aspect is terrifying; they gather up the eyes, they swallow them, they laugh.

On my knees at the door of their mother's bedroom I hear uttered in her sleep words of which I do not grasp the meaning. All, I think, are turned away from me; all close their souls to me. Mme C herself, I fear, has found me out and shuns me. Had I then attained to bliss only to see myself immediately separated from it and condemned to irremediable solitude? Our last-born child, who sleeps with the maid, starts to weep, and I do the same at the door against which I should like to dash out my brains. My two beloveds have left me, each on her own little skiff, Angela sailing bright oceans I shall never see, Margaret on her river of pus and ill humour. The twins are there, one at the prow, one at the stern. Whenever I approach they strike at me with their oars. The old Cooper woman in red velvet is on board too:

'Do you remember,' she asks me, 'the day I died?'

With her plump hand she strokes her daughter's face.

'Come here, Margaret, just come here, and for one last time let me look in you for that which I have never found.'

At last, here I am on board. The demons, baffled, cast crooked looks at me, recognising my power: I hold in my hands the eyes from which she will be able to hide nothing.

## *Confession*

I declare that on the morning of Sunday the 29th of August 1887 in our flat on the Rue Brey I killed my wife Margaret *née* Cooper daughter of another Margaret Cooper a prostitute and an unknown father my son Padoue and my daughter Marie my wife with a pistol shot in the head and a pistol shot in the stomach namely where there is nothing but blackness as for the children I cut their throats having no more ammunition in my pistol which is a relic of my wars and yet the door was never re-opened.

IV

WILDLIFE

# HILDA

THE DAY I left the Society for the Encouragement of Zoology I was offered one of the young panthers born in the Society's park; a creature I promptly named, I don't know why, Hilda.

When I say 'panther', that is not quite correct. Hilda is a selot from Karabakh, species *Selotis selotis Fischhorn*, called after the learned adventurer who discovered it. Selots are not much larger than ocelots, but they are sturdier and fiercer, or so it is said. Their fur is not so sought after, being of a dull brown that turns pale in winter.

The Society also offered me a leash of blue leather, a harness and a sort of muzzle, fearing that I should not be allowed to take Hilda out for walks without these curbs.

Though still a young cub Hilda nevertheless gave proof of a strength and vivacity seldom met with. At the Society's bun-fight (rather overloaded with rich foods) she jumped on the table and carried off a ham pie to the top of a display-cabinet.

In Karabakh the selots live in the trees, from which they drop down upon their prey. Hilda ate the ham and threw pieces of pie-crust to us with a puckering of her mouth that seemed to me to combine irony with satisfaction.

Hilda then came silently down from the cupboard and dug her claws into several pairs of trousers. Pollock, the permanent secretary to the Society, advised me to have them cut, as one does with domestic cats; the Society's vet would do me this service. Others spoke of little leather boots for her. There will never be any question of either.

Hilda and I left the Society building at seven o'clock. The sun had become vast and orange, and was drowning the trees and rooftops. Hilda seemed happy. She padded at my side with a light tread. I ought to say that I had not attached her lead.

In the course of this walk I gave thought to the life I should have with Hilda. I should know no peace, I told myself. It was not nervousness—though in following Hilda in the streets I experienced a certain tremor—nor was it an evil delight in being powerful and feared. But it would be a constant struggle, no doubt, and my sleep would always be light.

Hilda would perhaps strip me, I thought, of my dreams. At the moment when I was slipping into them I should hear her growl, because someone was approaching, because she was hungry, because faint visions were coming to her of Karabakh.

Oh, I bear no ill will towards the Society for Encouraging Zoology. I walk in our trimly kept streets in the dusty gold of evening with Hilda. It is a princely gift. When we pass children or dogs I grip Hilda by the scruff of her neck, which is already meaty. She growls and bristles at the sight of little strangers, but my firm hand on her neck calms her.

Hilda will grow. The smell of her coat and her breath will become unbearable, says Pollock. It will be necessary, even if her full-grown size is not great, to give her raw meat or living animals, rabbits, perhaps, or chickens that I must go and buy at I know not what price.

I see myself next year with Hilda in the mountains. There is still a little light near the horizon, though the time is approaching midnight. Hilda is drawing me towards the fields. She walks with a slinking gait, ears laid back. Tonight she devours several of this year's lambs. Tomorrow the shepherds will go out hunting, armed with pitchforks. But Hilda the Invisible is safe in my office.

But there are also fierce dogs, wolf-hounds, stationed in the mountains. When, the following night, we are so rash as to return, they will hunt Hilda to the end of the open country, seize her by the throat and tear her to pieces between them.

Another day, in the town, Hilda escapes my vigilance. A lorry runs over her. The police destroy her. Taxidermists carry her off, and I find her back at the Society's Museum, which has failed to recognise its progeny.

We have turned down my road. It is broad and bordered with trees. Hilda sniffs them. She sniffs the droppings and urine of dogs. Some children have been following us, sniggering, since the bridge, led by a man in a grey shirt. Hilda turns and growls. The children run away, and the teacher shrugs his shoulders.

At the entrance of my block of flats joy overwhelms me. I sit on a bench and Hilda lays her head on my knees. Hilda, before disaster strikes we shall have some glorious days! I don't know why, but scratching her under the chin I see her in my flat walking on her hind legs, bearing towards the dining room a wooden plate on which lies a bird, a white bird, cooked in a grape sauce. The grapes shine green on the plate.

Tears come to my eyes. Hilda bounds up the stairs, upturning everything as she goes, and while my tears flow she arrives, I think, at my door, goes in, and destroys for ever the little common sense I have left.

# LAMONT

## I

I MET Lamont—the boat-girl—the day before the death of my maternal grandfather. It was at the end of June. Lamont, the first time I saw her, was sitting on a chair tilted precariously against the wall of the kitchen. A noisy crowd was drinking and shouting in the sitting room—a crowd in which, I told Lamont without knowing anything about her, I had not managed to find a place. Lamont nodded. She too, she said, felt herself a stranger there.

Along came our hostess, whom I shall call Estelle, a red-haired girl with prominent breasts, in a white woollen dress with slit sides: queen among the bumble-bees.

'Oh, you're hidden away there, you two.'

Lamont smiled without showing her teeth. One of her canines, however, slightly misplaced, flashed for a brief instant.

'I understand: you're waiting for a lull. Well, they'll be leaving soon. The drink's running out. Will you come on to dinner with us?'

Lamont looked at me with a double flicker of her eyelids, and against my better judgement I promised to go with them—I didn't exactly know where. I hardly knew who they were, apart from Estelle, to whom one of my teachers had introduced me, and who took me up, I think, only because I wrote, or at least had written, for literary magazines.

Lamont gave a sardonic chuckle when Estelle had turned away.

'It's nothing to laugh about,' I protested. 'I've no great desire to stay with these people. I'd be better off at home.'

Lamont raised her shoulders and promised me a night of intense amusement. Did I know Boris, Estelle's sweetheart?

'Hardly,' I replied. Lamont rubbed her nose. She was a slight, flat-chested girl with short hair dyed ash-blond. Her eyes, under thick eyebrows, were almost black.

'Why stay here with these people we don't particularly like? Why not slip quietly away, just you and me, before it's too late?'

Lamont bit her lower lip. This time I saw both canines, small and pointed.

'Where would you like us to go?'

I saw myself walking not close to her, two or three steps behind, rather, looking at her back, looking at the shadow she cast on the pavement.

'I don't care. Wherever you like.'

She shook her head.

'I don't understand you,' I said. And I ought, at that moment, to have roused myself and said goodbye to both Lamont and Estelle, whom I should then never have seen again. We had no friends in common, we didn't even live in the same district. But I stayed. I had pleasure in talking with Lamont; that, I believed, would surely keep me safe throughout the evening from Estelle and her set.

From the kitchen we heard Estelle's pre-dinner guests take their leave. As Lamont understood it, Estelle was celebrating her birthday (twenty-third? twenty-fifth?) in several stages.

'And why does she want me? Do you think she needs some chance idiot to make up her dinner party? Do you think I'm going to have a fling with her?'

But before Lamont had time to reply, red-haired Estelle reappeared, hands clasped over her chest. 'Come and join us in the sitting room, you savages. The others have gone.'

In the sitting room of Estelle's little flat there remained only her friend Boris and two other guests I had not seen arrive. One of these was perfidiously introduced to me as 'a fifteen-year-old poet', the other, older than we, took in Lamont with a single glance and then shrugged his shoulders with an odd grimace—a signal directed more at me than at Lamont. I effaced myself. Boris went into the kitchen and brought back a bottle of excellent champagne and some paper cups. Estelle laughed, and Lamont watched her laugh.

When Lamont looked at me she was not so cruel. She looked often, more so than at the others. Later in the evening when we were walking down the street in search of a fashionable bar we never found, Lamont matched her step with mine, and in her company there came to me delicious images that at first I took for memories, until I realised they were more like waking dreams, fabrications my mind produced almost automatically under the influence of Lamont's presence. But before that she and I had had drinks in company with Estelle, and the oldest of Estelle's friends—not recalling his name I shall call him 'the Guru'; the young poet was called Hector—had spoken to me about post-Hegelianism and the 'melancholy of true philosophers'. And Lamont, while he was speaking, had never taken her eyes off him. Boris watched Lamont who watched the Guru; my eyes moved from one to another. And we had dined at an Italian restaurant in the Rue Notre Dame des Champs, where the Guru had given the second half of his lecture. But facing Lamont I was a child again, standing in front of a house of bricks, and a woman took me in her arms. Someone spoke to me. I had thought only for the house and the woman captured by my roving mind. It is certain, all the same, that I took part in the evening's debates. I was told afterwards of my tirades, which the Guru had found 'violently anticonceptual'.

'But do you know what philosophy is? Do you know what a system is?' I was asked at last by this psychagogue—as he was

called by the poet of fifteen years—speaking with brows raised
to the roots of his hair. We were installed in a private room at
the restaurant, where chandeliers and mirrors did their best to
compensate for the lack of windows; and uttering these words
the Guru pulled out from his waistcoat pocket a small leather
box and deftly rolled a doped cigarette. Friend Boris was not so
practised, and Lamont and I had an idiotic laugh. As for concepts, 'I am,' I confessed to the Guru, 'quite unable to manage
them.'

'You should learn. Anything can be learnt. You need a
teacher.'

The cigarettes passed from lips to lips. Neither Lamont nor I,
however, touched them. The Guru did not offer himself as a
teacher. His spectacles gleamed in the smoke. I heard the poet of
fifteen years reciting in impassioned tones one of his own works
to Lamont. Lamont allowed herself to chuckle sardonically.

Estelle was drunk. She had put her hand on my arm and was
letting her head nod, not daring to speak for fear of sliding
down the slippery slope of confessions and infidelities. On the
other side of the table the Guru, head bowed, was retailing his
adventures 'in the wild mountains of the Lebanon, realm of the
Druses and the Assassins'.

'Godlike Hashishins,' murmured the poet. Boris was dragging
at his third or fourth joint, and muttering insults to me in a low
voice. 'Do you expect to have your dinner paid for, you
sponger?' Lamont suddenly disappeared, and we did not see her
again till the moment for settling up. 'I'm going home,' I whispered in her ear. Estelle had slipped her arm under mine and
Boris under the influence of cannabis had landed her a vicious
slap. But once again Lamont gently shook her head. She needed
me; had I no desire to cross the town in such good company? I
closed my eyes and breathed in the heavy ripe scent of powder
on Lamont's hair.

At the till we each paid for ourselves. I wanted Lamont to be my guest, even though it would cost me, I reckoned, three days of service at the Murillo college, my source of bread and butter in those hard times. One of these days was sacrificed at The Inconvenient, a steamy establishment on the Rue Delambre, on the altar of 'Tangiers Kisses'—I do not know to this day what went into them—swallowed in the uproar. As the Guru, who could hardly hear himself speak, admitted, the 'late' bar was not a success. I drank other cocktails with crushed ice which plunged me into torpor. 'You're drinking too much,' said Boris, who was further gone, however, than I. No, it was not to me he was speaking. To whom, then? The poet, who soon went out to vomit. When he came back Estelle gave the signal for departure. 'Come on; now we'll all go to Boris's.' Lamont smiled broadly and put her hand on my neck. 'I really,' she said, 'must see this.'

'Lamont! At the stage we've reached!'

I do not have an accurate memory of Boris's flat—or rather the flat of his parents, who were away. I have never been back there. Nor do I remember Boris's face, though all evening I saw it wavering between Estelle and Lamont. Nor have I any better recollection of Boris's sister, who was waiting upon us, neither of her face, nor her name, nor her voice. And she twined herself around us all, a virgin vine with carnivorous leaves. Had we woken her up? Had Boris warned her in advance? I don't know. But in the large room in which we were installed and drank she never stopped walking to and fro, breathing noisily, muttering, casting upon us one after another furious glances of which we did not know what to think—except for the Guru, who eventually took her in his arms. It was four in the morning. The poet had fallen asleep on Lamont's knee with open eyes. The sister, seized with a spasm of trembling, put her hands over her groin and started a loud snuffling, until Boris went over and smacked her on each cheek.

'Come on, wake up, you're being a bore.'

'Boris, leave her in peace.'

'It's for her to leave us in peace. She's making an exhibition of herself.'

'I'm making an exhibition of your nothingness. You piss me off with your nothingness,' retorted the sister. I started to laugh. The sister disengaged herself from the Guru and staggered uncertainly. Tears flowed over her cheeks, down her neck into her corsage. She advanced towards me. Lamont wore her animal smile.

The sister kissed me on the mouth.

'In the past,' she sobbed, 'I have been disembowelled, cleaned out. Can't you feel it?' She took my hand, and made it slide beneath the belt of her skirt. 'Can you feel it or can't you?'

With the tips of my fingers I must have stroked the edges of her pubic hair. Alcohol then took control of me. I took the skin of her pubis between my thumb and forefinger and gave a sharp pinch. She screamed: 'Boris! Boris! Boris!'

Boris pushed me against the window of the room.

'Have you hurt her, you fucking bastard?'

'I've done nothing.'

'Bastard! Bastard! I'll have you arrested.'

But to my amazement I was bigger than Boris and certainly stronger. Over his elbow I saw the Guru consoling the sister. Estelle was asleep in her turn on the sofa. Of Lamont and the poet there was no trace. They had gone, they claimed later, to look for croissants. 'Lamont, you're pulling my leg.' They had not found any, and I have no recollection of any general reconciliation in the early morning. We left, Lamont and I, after the sun had risen. The sister, having been consoled by the Guru, who was drunk at last, set off in quest of a fresh drama. Estelle was snoring, and the three others once again manufactured their mystic cigarettes with the air of conspirators. They spoke of Guenon, of amnesia and of ecstasy, subjects suggested by Lamont, who had then quickly withdrawn from the conversation; she was disheartened, she said, by this fag end that travelled from mouth to mouth like a dead cockroach.

But in the early sun we were in a mood approaching joy. I proposed to Lamont that I should escort her home. She lived, by a happy chance, at Arcueil, near the autoroute.

'It's on my way,' I said.

We had a coffee at the Place Denfert-Rochereau. I had remembered a Café d'Orient which had replaced a restaurant that was shut in the morning. The pavements steamed.

'What would be fun would be to go home on foot, if you're up to it.'

In the light of day Lamont's appearance was changed. Her cheeks were fuller, but she put me in mind of a boy I had known, a passing friend who had once taught me to steal wallets in the Metro, an art I had only once put into practice. I told Lamont about it. She showed her teeth. I imagined her nude, sitting in a chair with her legs spread, and started to bleed at the nose. She laughed. And I wanted to go home on foot?

We went up the Avenue Coty and the deceptive slope of the Avenue Deutsch de la Meurthe. The night came back to me in all its drunkenness. 'Those people, Lamont, do you really know them?' Lamont had met Boris, Estelle's friend, at a second-hand record-shop: she worked as a saleswoman on Sundays. They had often spoken together. They had become friends. When he was on his own, Boris was not so brutish.

We crossed the park of the Cité Universitaire, which had just opened. The lawns were empty. Towards the bottom of the campus tiredness overtook me. Lamont, who was walking in silence, hands in the pockets of her jacket, regarded me with a novel compassion. 'I used to know that church,' I said, pointing at the fearsome angels of the church of Gentilly. Lamont lived a little further on. We walked beside the tracks of the RER, which at the meeting point of Arcueil and Gentilly crosses the Autoroute du Sud. Lamont explained that she was house-sitting for friends who had gone abroad. The french window of the kitchen, through which she made me come in, as she put it, for a 'refreshment', opened upon a small garden. Lamont, seated at the kitchen table, her face between the yellow walls reflecting the pale morning light, closed her eyes. I did the same. We slept for a quarter of an hour, facing one another across the table. The dream we had did not come back to me till later in the day, after my visit to my dead grandfather.

Lamont accompanied me back as far as the street.

'It can't be too pleasant,' I said, groping for something to say, 'living between the line to Sceaux and the autoroute.'

She smiled. She had the whole house to herself, paying only a 'peppercorn' rent. She chose this expression carefully.

Lamont wrote her telephone number in my notebook. The address I already knew, didn't I? I shook her hand—that too *faute de mieux*. But the skin of her face was so pale, so insubstantial, that it made me fear I should be kissing only emptiness.

II

My grandfather died that afternoon, one hour, I was told, before my arrival. 'We called your mother, but there was no reply.' My mother had gone to Italy with her second husband. The nurse took me to my grandfather's room—a different room from the one he had occupied for the last two months. The blinds were lowered. My grandfather was lying on his bed, the arms spread apart a little from the body, and his mouth wide open.

'Someone will come and close it, sir. Don't you worry.'

The woman left me alone, and I passed my hand over my grandfather's cheek, which was still warm—something at least above the temperature of the room—still warm and soft, so much so that I bent over to kiss it. In the passage I started to cry. My tears fell on the linoleum, squeezed out by my tiredness as much as by true grief. The nurse took me back to the waiting room and offered me coffee. In my mind's eye I saw Lamont again, her face almost translucent in the morning light, her eyes fathomless, her elbows on the kitchen table. I nearly telephoned her from the hospital to tell her about my grandfather with his mouth open upon its dead interior, an open mouth I ought never to have seen.

'Is it the first dead person you have seen?' asked the nurse.

I had already seen my two grandmothers and a young motor-cyclist, the top of his skull broken open. But it was my mother I called, not Lamont. My mother and her husband came back to France next day and took charge of everything.

Nevertheless, the same evening, when I had gone to bed and was torn with spells of grief, the dream returned to me that I had had in Lamont's kitchen—the dream I dreamt along with Lamont. It was like this. After having offered me a cup of coffee Lamont stood up and signed to me to follow her. We went out of the kitchen. The rest of the house smelt of saltpetre. Lamont opened a door that gave onto the stairs to the basement, a white clean room lit by a naked bulb. Next, another door, another room, and then a small bathroom. Lamont sat down on the cover of the lavatory and seated me upon the rim of the bath. She raised her arms upwards, and I rose precipitately. A man's body, cut in pieces and neatly skinned, was arranged in the bath. Lamont moved me aside with an affectionate gesture, turned on the hot tap. The steaming water flowed over the pieces of the man, whose head was placed face down between his two bare feet. We both awoke at this moment and looked at each other in a quandary by the yellow light of the kitchen.

I often saw Lamont in Paris, and almost always took her back to her door; but I never again went into her house, or rather into the house of her friends, if they really existed. She invited me once or twice. I refused under various pretexts; and she did not speak of it again. Lamont, now that I reflect on it, plunged me into a blissful stupor. I walked close to her; I often brushed against her hand or her thigh inadvertently; her shoulders stiffened; and a chill spread through my legs. In these moments of weakness memories came to me—something I had experienced since that first night—memories which I took for my own, but which perhaps were only inventions by Lamont. These fragments were hard to pin down: lost worlds, pounded up in Lamont's brain.

Then she left Paris for the United States. She had an uncle there or a cousin—I forget which—who could provide for her and give her a final year at university. What she was studying, how she really lived, I have never known and I never asked. She gave me an address in Portland, Oregon, and I went with her to the airport. The house in which she had once received me, the house in which we had slept and dreamed together, remained, so far as I could see, empty.

As for Estelle, she gave no sign of life until she visited me one September evening shortly after Lamont's departure, in the small house which I left a month later for my grandfather's flat in Paris. In the autumn I was still living at Plessis-Robinson in this little damp cabin at the bottom of a garden; a clump of withered lilacs grew under my window. The evening when Estelle came I was slightly out of sorts, trying to write a letter to Lamont. I wanted to be amusing, but could not bring it off. I was lying fully dressed on the bed, my letter on my chest, a book with a hard cover within reach. On the ceiling I saw shadows passing, a flotilla of them, trembling waves: but neither Lamont nor me among them.

Someone tapped on the window pane. From the bed I saw my neighbour's son making a face.

'Hi there?'

When I opened the window he told me two girls were looking for me, and he hadn't liked to let them into the garden. They were waiting in the street, the noses of both of them blue with cold. One was Estelle, the other a slightly younger girl, a lithe brunette. I have forgotten her name, so I shall call her Laure. Laure was standing on the pavement beating her hands together. Estelle, a violet-coloured woollen bonnet pulled over her eyes, asked me if she could finish her cigarette. I made them come into the house; on the threshold Estelle, I think, experienced a sort of tremor. 'The smell of poverty,' I said to myself, only to remember that the phrase came straight from one of the conversations that night between Boris and the Guru.

I offered them tea, and I no longer have the least idea what we chatted about: Boris, perhaps, or our various occupations; possibly of Lamont, whom Laure did not know. Laure kept looking at her watch and the toes of her boots. Estelle, after several efforts, asked me what I had in the way of music. Didn't I have some Sufi stuff? The Guru, I eventually understood, had taken them off to hear the Dervishes of Lower Egypt. Laure gave an audible sniff. Distant cousin of Estelle, she knew neither the Guru nor the young poet—but Estelle, oh yes, she'd always known her. And what was 'always' for this pair of geese? There was a moment when, with the two girls standing against the wall and regarding me with curiosity and, I then fancied, some disgust, I felt myself slipping into the pure darkness of Lamont's cellar. My eyes saw in front of them the fresh faces of the two innocents, and behind them—or so I suppose—the subterraneous regions of Lamont's house.

That did not last, Laure looked again at her watch and I said that, true enough, it was late.

'Ah, you're right.'

Docilely they resumed their coats, their hats, their gloves.

'And you say,' babbled Estelle in her high-pitched voice, 'that Lamont is now living in America?'

The girl I call Laure kept silent.

I escorted them to the Robinson Metro station. In the forecourt Laure gave me her hand, her eyes elsewhere. Estelle moved away, shook her head, then took off her bonnet and turned to me.

'You know, we're not going to be able to go back to Paris right away.'

'Estelle, listen,' said Laure. 'It's idiocy. Don't you see it's complete idiocy? We're off. Drop it.'

Estelle stared at me with eyes that were suddenly tragic. Darkness was coming on. Chattering groups emerged at intervals from the station.

'We have to return to your house.'

'You haven't left anything behind, so far as I know.'

'Yes we have,' said Estelle, 'in a way.'

'Explain yourself.'

Laure hid her face in her gloved hands.

'You remember my birthday party?' said Estelle. 'You remember the party at my flat? After that party' (her voice took on a curious hoarseness) 'someone rifled the bowl I keep my jewellery in. It's all gone. You . . . you understand? We don't know each other all that well.'

'We don't know each other at all,' I replied. 'What do you think? That I've laid my hands on your bloody jewels? You've come to demand them back from me? You stupid cow! Do you really believe that I'd hand them back politely after having stolen them?'

Lights flickered in the sky from an aeroplane passing above the station.

They returned to my house with downcast eyes, and while Laure and I played cards—we had to pass the time somehow—the shame-faced Estelle ransacked the little house from top to bottom. I saw her even empty the washing machine, which was full of dirty underwear, and open my rubbish bins. There formed in my stomach a fury which made me want to hit this girl, this Estelle, until she bled. The other girl, Laure, would certainly have lent me a hand.

At last I got them out of the door. Once or twice, as I watched them, I had pondered absently on the best way of killing them. I had once, for a moment, seen young Laure pinned to the ground under the skinning knife without my raising a finger. 'Who will come looking for them at my place? They've told no one of their stupid plan.'—'No' said the voice of reason; 'there's my neighbour's son, he has seen them,' and I added the boy to my list of victims.

One or two weeks passed before I was able to tell Lamont about the two silly girls. I wrote two or three letters a week to her, but I did not post them all. Lamont was lazier. She sent postcards: sea lions from the Seattle aquarium, avalanche lilies, bears standing on their hind legs, holding fish in their jaws, large red and black totem poles belonging to Indians on the Pacific coast, cherry blossom festivals. Her messages had a lapidary quality. She worked for three months in Portland, then found a job and a flat-share in Tacoma. I moved into my grandfather's place. My mother and her husband had bought out the other heirs, and leased it to me for six hundred francs a month. In this flat I set myself almost every night to dream with greater or less vividness of Lamont. They were often amorous dreams, with Lamont making me absurd propositions. She was naked, sitting in the grass, the blades of which marked her buttocks and her knees; she was outstretched in mud, in water, her face just emerging from its smooth surface; she was smiling, putting her tongue out at me, raising her knees. I was going to join her. The dreams probably made me stray from the life I should have been leading. My days and my companions seemed equally misty. At this period I was working in a shop selling scientific books on the Boulevard Richard-Lenoir, and under my negligent direction it was dying of inanition. The owner, a victim of early dementia, used to come every evening, when I first worked for him, and disarrange the books; next morning it was my task to reorder them. In the end he threw himself under a Metro train. I found work a couple of stops further, in a shop that sold works in foreign languages. We often went to lunch at La Grisette, the shop girls and I—they were two girls, one undulating, the other short and chubby. I never spoke to them of Lamont.

## III

The dreams in which Lamont appeared to me were not all erotic. Some nights she—or the inexact likeness which my dreaming brain substituted for her—received me in her home, in a middle class flat. Her husband would greet me coldly, and a child, sometimes a girl, sometimes a boy, would grasp me by the leg. Or we would go to a concert together, and lose sight of each other during the interval. I was never happier than during this period in my life, which is the reason it never occurred to me to join Lamont in America. Did Lamont on her side dream of me with the same assiduity? I never asked her. I sometimes had the foolish feeling, however, that we were making some of our dreams together. There was really a moment in the night, wasn't there, that we shared? Then Lamont, as once in Paris, would sit close to me and draw from my head memories that were not mine. It would have been ideal, of course, to go to sleep at the same times as she, so that she would have the opportunity to dig down to the bottom of my mind.

It was the poet aged fifteen (or sixteen or seventeen, for all I know) who dragged me against my will out of this amorous dizziness. One day towards the end of August I saw him enter the shop on the Boulevard Richard-Lenoir, and I recognised him as he consulted a French-Portuguese dictionary and furtively noted on a scrap of paper the word he was looking for. I coughed. He raised his eyes, blushed, and came over to me with outstretched hand. 'How *are* you? Do you work here? Ah, it's so quiet.' He had improved in looks, and was carrying by a shoulder strap a bag full of books. So what was he looking for? 'Oh, just a word. You know. . . .' The sales girls were out, one at a rendezvous, the other on holiday, and he established himself tranquilly on my side of the till.

'You've seen any more of those people? Boris de —, the professor?'

I shook my head. Hector deposited his bag under the counter, and I gave him a cup of coffee.

'I have some little cakes I've just bought. Would you like a little cake?

We shared the packet.

'It's odd,' said Hector. 'I haven't seen them since that evening of disgusting drunkenness—on the part of Boris's sister. Funny girl, don't you think? In point of fact I *have* seen Boris, but only in the distance, you know, and I ran across his sister, when was it, a month ago, yes, in July; and she told me he'd just gone off to America, to Seattle, to see that girl again. You know who I mean? What was she called?'

'Lamont,' I said, feeling the hand of death.

'And then his sister told me he was no longer with Estelle, and besides Estelle had completely vanished from circulation.'

'Estelle?'

'Yes.'

'But how is it that you came to know these people?'

'My sister went out with Boris, a long time ago. It didn't last. Between you and me, he's a real shit. But last year I wasn't on bad terms with him, I admit. A mistake of youth.'

'And Professor Machin?'

'Oh, him? He's Boris's spiritual guide, you might say. Actually he's no more a professor than you or me. He's in Israel at the moment, I think refuelling himself in a kibbutz.'

I steered the poet gently out of the door after we had eaten the cakes and drunk the coffee. I had the heart-rending conviction that the boy's indiscretion was going to drive Lamont from my dreams, never to return. Already I found myself unable to recreate her in my mind, to make her live in the tinsel theatre of waking imagination. And as I feared, she disappeared from that day forward. My dreams were always quite varied, always distributed quite unpredictably in my nights, but other girls than she played in the little charades of my unconscious. The poet, blundering fool, had plucked the flower of my dreams.

I went on writing to Lamont, but I never had the courage to ask her if what the poet had said was true. And I received two cards in reply, one showing the beach at La Push, the other Douglas firs on Mount Olympus. Had she visited those mountains in company with Boris? Jealousy devoured me, slowly eating away the whole interior of my body. I used to go to the bookshop as an empty shell, and gave myself up, when the others had their backs turned, to sterile rage. The sales girls found me changed and tried to cheer me up; they often invited me to dinner at La Grisette. I remember one evening when, after one of these therapeutic dinners, I went back to my place on foot. It was an astonishingly cold night. I lived on the slopes, near the Jourdain Metro station. I saw the moon, evilly bloated, detach itself from the roofs and float slowly up in a slightly misty sky. Why love Lamont only from afar? And being unable to remember accurately either her features or those of Boris, I could picture to myself on the slopes of Mount Olympus nothing but the grotesque couplings of monsters without heads.

I wanted to see once again the house at Arcueil. It was probably later in the year, a Sunday morning. I went back by the route I had followed with Lamont, through the campus of the Cité Universitaire, and past the front of the Portuguese church, the angels of which were perhaps reformed demons, fired in bronze and then rapidly hauled up, by way of punishment, above the Boulevard Péripherique; nothing escaped their malign gaze. The one that looked towards the south saw me at its feet take the Rue Malon and follow the track of the RER. But at the entry of the Passage Boutet the angel's eye transfixed the back of my neck. Grief nailed me to the wall. With an irresistible iron blade it calmly opened up my back, rolled back the skin and the covering of muscles, and in despite of me, fabricated a pair of wings for my shoulders. 'You understand, my friend? You are one of us.' Before me I saw appear Boris's sister, whose name I had forgotten. 'I show you the spectacle of your nothingness, and my rage before your nothingness.' She approached, arms extended, sex exposed. I went on my way; I had recovered my strength.

Lamont sent me from Boise in Idaho a card showing peaks one above another. She had found a winter season job in a mountain hotel, 'perfectly modern' she wrote. I should have liked to explain to her the company in which I found myself, but it was impossible. The angel of the South tore the pen from my hands. What haunted me above all was Boris, subtle beast; Boris in a mountain hotel with long corridors hung with bull's blood paper, a potted plant or a spittoon every two yards—Boris opening the thousand doors of the hotel upon the sleeping Lamont. I arranged another meeting with the young poet. He was my path to the sister, and the sister to Boris, even if this familial logic seemed to me increasingly tortuous. It was not hard to make the young poet talk, on his guard as he was. I invited him to come after opening hours to a bar on the Rue du Faubourg du Temple, and I made him drink first wine and then whisky. 'I find extraordinarily trite the idea of a poet who drinks,' he said, 'the idea in general that one can find inspiration only in sorrow and absence. I wish to write of joy.'

That was now, he confided to me with shining eyes, his 'new project'. Armed with his accursed passion for the positive, he kept beating for a good hour around the bush—in which the former love of Boris for Estelle had been conceived. Or of Estelle for Boris.

'For the last time, Hector. You've told me either too much or too little.'

The little wretch gave an embarrassed laugh.

'I've thought about it. It's better, as you say, to speak out, to probe the abscess. Boris from the first day took a total dislike to you. Is that what you felt? Yes, you could call it a morbid hatred. He was furious that Estelle had asked you to her birthday. He went so far as to wonder if you and Estelle were not sleeping together. He pocketed Estelle's jewellery, and made her believe that you were responsible.'

'What a slimy creep,' I said. And the poet, soon to be an adult, ordered a second whisky and drank it neat at one gulp.

'And you, Hector, what did you think? That I was sleeping with Estelle? That I was too seedy for her? That I had stolen her filthy jewels to pay myself back for the evening?'

'I don't know anything,' said the cautious booby. 'I'm no judge of people.'

'And Lamont, poet? Where does she come from?'

Lamont, thought the poet, his tongue running on faster than ever, was a friend of Boris. 'You didn't know? You fancied her, all the same?'

Excess of alcohol made him explicit. There came to me, while he shut his eyes and massaged his chin, a luminous idea, a deliverance. Boris had not gone to America to join Lamont. But from here in Paris, and to humiliate me—the reason for this persecution I still couldn't grasp—he was sending his tormentors. The poet drank a third whisky which I was so kind as to offer him.

'And you say that Estelle has left France too?'

'She isn't anywhere any more,' the poet replied with a look of vague unease.

## IV

I dreamt again of Lamont, now that I had driven her seducer
from my mind. My time without her had been almost three
months. Lamont came back the second or third day after I had
hocused the young poet. In the dream that restored her an old
gipsy had me visit her garden, in which were playing some
deformed children. That was caused, she said, by the high
tension wires. Lamont was waiting for me, sitting on the verge;
from here she could see both the old woman's garden and the
lake in which other children were paddling among weed. There
was no effusion of joy in the dream, at least my dreaming self
had no consciousness of it. But I woke in the night for no
apparent cause and knew that I had again found her whom I
loved. I saw myself drifting down in the darkness, a pale raft,
with Lamont lying stretched out on top of me, and trailing her
hand through the water, her strange smile on her lips.

Lamont, oh bliss, was no longer confined to dream; after that
night she came to me also at certain moments in the day, and
soon in order to see her or feel her near me I had no need even
to be alone or sleepy. She often came when I was working in the
bookshop, and, invisible as she was, entwined herself with me
and looked out at the customers or my too curious colleagues
through my eyes; and when I shut them, something I never did
without careful precautions, I was alone with her, alone with
Lamont, and could hear her moving about within my body.
Occasionally, and this could happen at any hour of the day or
night, whether or not I was alone, she would grasp hold of my
buttocks, and I would see on the plump swelling of her lower lip
her two small canines. If by good fortune I was alone at these
moments I withdrew into myself, I found my Lamont, I let my
joy in her wash over me. This so to speak luminous and shining
body of Lamont I now carried through the streets with a

renewed pride, and I think I pitied those who could not see me. It seemed to me I could have made these insensates feel my happiness with their fingers. Sometimes shadows would issue from my sleeves, and I would make them enact scenes of my life with and without Lamont: that was when I was alone with her, and it would make us writhe in laughter. But why not speak of it to everyone, beginning with those around me? 'No,' I said to Lamont, 'if they do not see this brilliance, what can we do?' And she, delectable cannibal, nibbled the lining of my stomach while I continued to tell lies to the unbelievers, and fell asleep with her head in my burning entrails.

Thereafter I no longer saw the world except through a two-way grill which allowed particles of light to escape—but not enough to make those who still lived around me scatter, transformed by fear. No, there was no fear, and I went forward masked. People came to me, even, and asked me what news I had of the poet and other persons. The poet walked a path I did not know. But I was unwilling to say I had sent him away, and that on this road that had neither beginning nor end there also wandered other souls. Neither beginning nor end nor the faintest light, whereas I could produce it through every pore in my glorified body.

Setting out from the town early and while it was still dark, I have walked without meeting anyone; the magnificent fire beneath my skin is extinguished at sunrise, and this has caused me not distress but lightness of heart. 'Have I still bones? Have I still a skin?' 'Obviously, idiot, since you are walking.' My skin— and this makes me laugh, and spread out my arms—my skin actually separates two worlds; I am the living frontier. 'Come on, come on,' I should like to say to those who pass me in the morning; but not one of them thinks of treading on me, digging into my skin, and passing with amazement to the other side where nevertheless, I could assure them, all is light. I brush against them, laughing, drunkenly or soberly depending on who is looking at me. For old women I have a drunken eye, for the strong a beatific smile and extended hand. I pass beneath the four angels. Eight hands, eight rough feet of bronze, push me towards the house in the Passage Boutet; I am miniscule between their colossal legs. Boris is sitting at the kitchen table, and the golden yellow paint of the walls gives the skin of his face the shine of baked bread. He rises when I enter, he carries his hands to his mouth. I sign to him to be silent. He recoils anxiously, knocking over the chair. I shake my head and hold out my hand to him. He raises his eyes to the ceiling. Perhaps he thinks we are not alone. He comes forward, he comes towards me, and I withdraw, bowing, laughing up my sleeve. Boris's hands take me by the waist. A step towards the door to the basement. Boris draws me towards him; I laugh soundlessly, pretending to resist him.

We cross the threshold. Boris goes down first, and I shut the door before joining him in the dark. 'Turn on the light,' comes his voice, suddenly mistrustful. The same bulb illuminates the same white walls, the same low door which Boris opens briskly, but there is nothing and no one in the further room, still whiter and more empty than the first.

'There,' I say. 'Come.'

Boris is seated on the edge of the bath, his hands on his knees. We are both stark naked, and Boris, holding with one hand his stiffening penis, caresses the skin of my arm and murmurs 'Lamont, sweet Lamont, you are burning bright inside here.'

'Your return is my happiness,' he says, and tips up into the bath. Pressing down with all my weight on his shoulders, I strangle him, happy Boris, and I shall later make him pass, piece by piece, like the others, into that other country of which I am the frontier.

# FERAL

BY DAY the dull red front of the house is switched off; by night, in contrast, lit by a lamp on the pavement, it rears up high and devours the street, which in Kim's time bore the name Avenue de la Neva. Two alleyways led off it at right angles to an empty plot along the track of the RER B. Travelling circuses of no great importance used to camp there. Once, perhaps, there had been a tiger that the clatter of passing trains drove into a frenzy. Otherwise, there were at best horses, and when they struck camp there lingered the smell of horse-dung and of wagons purveying pizza.

Kim lived there until her twentieth year. She smoked her first cigarette in that derelict space one winter, when it snowed for more than a week. From the bridge over the motorway you could see the cars crawling slowly under a violet sky, white lights moving north and red moving south. Kim threw down over the railing without regret the stub of her second cigarette, which she hadn't finished. The following evening, snow having brought the trains to a halt, she took back to the silence of the area two boys from her class, and as a new form of baptism drank a bottle of vodka with them, she swallowing the last of it at one gulp. With these boys and with others she used often, before she reached the age of eighteen, to slip under the barrier and go drinking on the slope that ran down to the motorway: in winter it was completely bare, in summer, like the country.

Twice they were rewarded, so to speak, by the spectacle of an accident: once a car smashing into a lorry—that was terrifying—and later a pile-up in which some vehicles exploded.

At about this time Kim acquired the habit of lying on her back and looking at the sky, not for its own sake but because there appeared before her retina the cells, floating in the vitreous humour, clear and gelatinous, of her eyeballs, and in following their movements she eventually saw the interior of her own eyes—or so, at least, she thought. In this way she passed insensate hours looking into herself, not only on the edge of the motorway, but also during her lessons and even in her room in the morning and at night, where the corpuscles became invisible.

A little later, when she was a student, she followed an itinerary: over the motorway (the same one, though she no longer had time to go down there), then along beside the tracks of the RER, finally crossing the ring road by a footbridge that led over it into the park of the Cité Universitaire. From there she took the Metro—on some days she turned off in the vicinity of the footbridge or more rarely in the park. There were signs that encouraged her to abandon her journey, puddles of a particular shape on the paths that reflected, not the trees, but other forms it was better not to recognise, and menacing looks from statues. Kim, rather unenterprisingly, was studying biology at Jussieu, near the Jardin des Plantes.

'Everything depends on monkeys,' she said to herself, standing before Cambodia House, which was guarded by simian deities, their foreheads low, their legs spread out. 'One day they will announce the end of time.'

Time went on nevertheless, Kim pursuing her way towards Paris and returning in ill humour either by Gentilly—Rues Malon, Thélémine—or Champs Elysées.

There came a night when, her parents being away, she left their house and sat down naked on the pavement, facing so as to see with a fresh eye the blood red façade. She went down towards the motorway using her old routes, and walked towards Paris without meeting a single car. Walking through the tunnel which passed beneath the park of the Cité Universitaire terrified her. The skin dissolved on her flesh. At the far side, she hastened to regain the streets, the open air. At the Avenue de la Neva a neighbour's cockerel greeted her return. Her feet were bleeding and she slept for hours. After this expedition she never went again to the University. The sullen seriousness she had hitherto devoted to her studies was lost in the tunnel; or in the dance she executed on the footbridge when she was returning.

To disguise her absenteeism, she adopted the well-tried device of continuing to leave home at her usual times. She soon discovered three different routes. At the bottom of the town a concrete cover sealed off the underground course of the Bièvre; you passed through a doorway, sometimes open, and walked alongside the river. Then, at Montsouris there was a fabulous ravine that crossed the park from east to west, the line of la Petite Ceinture, for many years disused. Finally, not far from the towers of Jussieu, there was the Alpine Garden of the Jardin des Plantes, to which again there was access by a tunnel.

Oh, that first night, crouched beneath a tree at the furthest end of the small gorge that constitutes the Alpine garden! It must have been her third or fourth visit there. The weather was bad, and she was alone. She crept under the chain that shut off the end of the ravine. The whistle-blasts signifying the closure of the garden sounded out. She was not pursued, although at every stridulation her heart leaped with a sharp thump that sounded to her like a clicking tongue. Night came on; she dared to hold up her head and sniff the air. It smelt of large carnivores, or perhaps of kangaroos, whose enclosure was next to the Garden. Further off there was the chatter of night birds. She pissed in the bushes and ate a *pain au chocolat* that some urchin had thrown over the barrier. A half-moon rose, and she followed its movement avidly. On later nights she let herself be shut in other gardens.

'I'm sleeping at a girlfriend's house,' she would tell her parents.

She no longer had friends, however, something to which she did not give so much as a thought.

CR

'I'll take the plunge in the spring,' she said to herself one rainy evening which she spent in the streets, walking continually because the cold made her afraid to go to sleep.

She went round the dustbins, she tried eating the remains of a sandwich, and was surprised that she experienced no disgust in partaking of the germs and saliva of a complete stranger. At about four in the morning she crossed the Seine by the big bridge, smooth and white, that links the Gare de Lyon and the Gare d'Austerlitz. The rain had turned to snow. She walked down the middle of the road, ruler of all she surveyed. It remained only to choose the place. She put the rest of the winter to good use in constructing a map. The principal entrance, she was sure, would be at Montsouris. Several times, eluding the watchmen, she went down into the gorge through which ran the tracks of the disused railway. She spent two nights there. On the second she went into the tunnel, although she didn't have a torch. The darkness had tendrils. They clutched at her legs, her arms, her neck, they sucked her courage, they released her at the far end laughing, weakened, but apparently intact.

She ran away in the last days of April. Her parents had just left for Argentina on a two weeks' holiday to celebrate their silver wedding anniversary. They left the house in her care. Kim went with them to the RER station; all three were in excellent spirits. She was, in fact, like someone drunk and out of her mind, but managed to conceal this from them. That afternoon she in turn packed her bag, taking a knife, a sleeping bag and a few provisions. She also stowed a little money, which she never used, and stout shoes. She went off on foot to the park, crossing the bridge over the motorway (with a prayer for the dead) and then the footbridge by Cambodia House (with a prayer to the simian kings that ruled their temples). Some weeds had been burnt there a few days before. She paused for a moment to watch the traffic on the ring road, —red, white, red, white—and to look at the four angels of the Portuguese church, and she took care to pay her respects to the monkeys. Similarly at Montsouris, before slipping furtively past the barrier, she genuflected before a group of lion-cubs in bronze at the bottom of the park—strangled, she recalled, by a hydra.

The descent was steep. She had to cling to tufts of grass and branches in order not to fall. She lay down beside the railway tracks. The sky stayed blue for a full hour; then it yellowed before passing into the usual grey cotton wool of towns. The blood in Kim's veins turned black.

'Ah,' she thought, 'this way I shall not die.'

The thought thrilled her. The city above could perish in ruin; she, Kim, would survive in its rotting guts. One day she would re-emerge, the last of womankind.

⊗

She established herself for the night in a shelter in the tunnel which had harboured other drop-outs before her. There were bottles, empty tins of food and a strange smell which was not, as she had dimly feared it would be, that of urine. She herself pissed and shat that evening on the tracks, her knees shaking. She wiped herself with a paper handkerchief and buried it beneath pieces of hoggin. Back in the shelter she slowly explored with her index finger the valley between her legs, from the puckered mouth of her anus to the lips of her vulva, which she stroked absently. Next day she applied herself to hunting.

She had slept late, understanding that from now on she would have to live at night. There were water-points along the line, used by others besides herself. Her provisions being exhausted in a few days, she killed pigeons and rats by throwing stones, drank their blood and ate their tiny hearts, their livers and their lights, and as much of their flesh as she could detach from the bones. In late evening she would go out up into the park and rummage through the dustbins. But she did not allow her new kingdom to go to her head, especially as she was sharing it with others as elusive as herself. The railway line was home to all sorts of outcasts. Their fires burnt in the tunnels, villages of cardboard arose out of nothing. Kim picked a careful way between the encampments. Eventually she found a new hiding-place. To reach it you had to scale a wall of dressed stone five or six metres high: it was a real eagle's nest from which she could contemplate the tracks at her ease.

From rat's blood she tried to make herself gloves, rubbing it into her fingers and palms in the hope that the pigment would eventually impregnate her skin. When she went to wash in the lake of the Montsouris park it all came off. The blood attracted swans. One night she trapped one and wrung its neck before it could peck her. She carried it back to the shelter, plucked it—no easy task—and devoured all that she could find between the bird's ribs. The feathers she put on one side, and the beak and feet she later buried near the railway line. At that time she was still afraid to cook her prizes; the fire would have made her visible.

She also killed one of the ducks in the park and an owl that one morning had been so imprudent as to perch at the entry to her nest. She killed both by throwing stones; she had become expert. Sleeping during the day, she often dreamed of a vast city built on a hill of yellow grass and crossed by a valley. It was the yellow, speckled with brown and red, which you see in peat-bogs. She would walk there for hours, or perhaps for the minutes or seconds of her dream, constantly chewing the raw heart of some bird, or any other organ she pulled out of her prey without properly noticing it; and she would gnaw the bones and sometimes, even, she could not stop herself from swallowing them.

'What have you got in your stomach?'

'A rat's head.'

In her waking life she kept these things in a pile, and the feathers likewise; skulls and beaks that she washed in the water of the lake and anything else that wouldn't rot.

She was taken by surprise, during the first two months, by the onset of her period; the blood ran down her thighs for two or three days. She was by then going almost naked; it was a hot summer. In the autumn the bleeding ceased.

CR

At night she hunted in the park, then along the track which she learnt to skirt with caution, the human population there being dense. Better organised than she, they slept at night after their suppers beside their wood fires, which lit up their faces, espied by her from a distance. She never stole from them, having acquired a taste for raw meat and for spoilt fruit from the park dustbins. Two or three tunnels further on, however, there were rabbit warrens and kitchen gardens, and sheds for drying tomatoes and curing sausages. To the north west there was a chicken-coop with eggs and chickens. She turned herself into a fox. She strung out the skulls of her captures on the rails.

A little later she wanted to work on skins: her own to start with, and then those of the animals she hunted. She slid under her skin the smallest bones of birds and rabbits, first on one arm and then the other. That took her to the beginning of winter, a period she dated from when she had to go into winter quarters. The pain warmed her; several times she thought she was dying of cold or of various infections, something she viewed with indifference, despite the promise she had made to herself to die long after the rest of the world. As for the animal skins, she scraped them with her knife, then tenderised them on stones; but in spite of her efforts they hardened and became unusable. In the park dustbins she found plastic sacks in which she was obliged to clothe herself on top of the clothes she had preserved from the summer. The cold chapped her hands and lips. One evening she caught a fair-sized dog which she managed to kill cleanly. She ate its heart and liver the first day, having bled it after killing it; other unidentified organs she ate on the second day, and the meat of its thighs and rump on the third. She buried what was left in the park under a tree. The head, however, she preserved, after taking out the brain and the eyes, which she felt no desire to swallow. Insects picked the skull clean in a few days. The following week she had another dog, smaller, with short legs. After that, anything was fair game: cats, weasels. She wouldn't have been surprised to come up against a bear or a wild boar; in other towns, it was said, they were common. For the dogs she made a cross in the hollow of her thumb. That did not last, and she had to cut again and enlarge the incision with a little earth. She had a vague hope that horns and fur would grow on her: that too happens in other places. The third dog was young, its coat short and black. Since she did not know how to tan the hides, she kept it alive to warm her feet. It stayed with her. Dogs will eat dogs and many other things. This one, like her, slept by day, and never barked.

℘

It snowed. The dog brought in dead rats and a living cat she had to finish off. The first night of snow they went into the park and helped themselves to a couple of geese. The dog ate the head of the larger one then and there. Through the grill of the park gates she saw cars, their wheels spinning silently. When they went down again, the birds in her bag, the dog at her heels, she smelt the whiff of the fires that had been lit by the other inhabitants of these depths. A good thing, this snow; you could drink it, it added brightness to the night, and it kept fresh the meat of the animals you killed. She licked the horrible sores on her hands, she ate the scabs and clots of blood, which it was better not to offer to the dog. Yes, let the snow swallow up everything, let it engulf the city and those who dwell in it.

But that still did not come to pass. On particularly cruel nights she crept closer to the fires, despite everything, in order not to die. One of the shelters caught alight. The men who lived there had time to get out, shouting and throwing handfuls of snow on the brazier. She, pressed against the wall, was warm for once. Another evening she managed to steal two blankets from a garden: they had been put out to dry. It was at a place, far from her nest, where she could hear the roar of the motorway, as in former days. She stole some home-made preserves that she found in the garden shed, which made her sick: she had lost the habit of eating cooked food. In a garden on the way home she found a hen and two eggs, which she shared with the dog that kept her feet warm and cleaned her face and hands. The rest of her body was caked in filth.

The weather became milder for a few days, then returned to extreme cold. The dog one morning scented a dead body in the snow, a woman older than Kim, clad in overalls, a sweater and an anorak; these were removed with care and stored in the shelter. The dog chewed at her ribs; Kim covered up the body with snow. The woman was also wearing a camisole and pants. A woman of the tunnel, perhaps? Had she died in her sleep? of cold?

Kim had confused dreams. She was in an aeroplane, flying over a desert of ice. The aeroplane came down on the sea. She was the sole survivor, floating on top of the cockpit in the middle of the Pacific, or at least in some warm sea, ploughed by many ships which all altered their courses to come to her aid. A woman then folded her in her arms calling her 'my daughter'. She, however, was certain it was not her mother.

That evening, the snow unmelted, she came down from her nest, the dead woman's shoes on her feet. The corpse was still there beneath its covering of snow. The dog wagged its tail, panting. She cut off cleanly the cheeks and the flesh of the arms; she opened the abdomen and gave the liver to the dog; then swiftly re-covered the woman with snow. Having eaten, she went back up into the park hoping to find, in place of the dirty streets and harsh lights of the city, a true desert like that in her dream. She was disappointed, of course. She descended once more and went off with the dog along the railway line she now explored less often. Several times she found herself thinking of the body, and those parts of it that were still intact: the lungs, and above all the legs; soft legs and thighs. These she cleaned the two following evenings before burying what was left of the woman as far as possible from her nest.

Fresh dreams, or perhaps not dreams. First the dog, which ate three fingers of her left hand, something that in the end might actually happen. Then something seated itself over her eyes with such force that they were driven into her brain. The cells of her retina, jumbled in disorder, bored into the grey matter, silent witnesses to the destruction of her spirit. Blindness was coming down on her. The migrating eyes re-emerged from her mouth. She died twice or three times. No, she did not die, she woke up in a limp chill. The other woman: was she really beneath the ground? When hunting with the dog she could not find the place where they had hidden the carcass.

Some days, scratching her head among the feathers and the imperfectly tanned hides, she saw herself entering into the dark perspectives of the dog. Or he into hers. Of what did he think, or dream? They went off to kill rabbits. The transmutation failed to occur. Her skin remained hairless; the ways open before her remained many. She thought of disappearing into the ground or into the lake, easy to do in this season of great hunger. Or should she depart from the city? But by what means? Or leave the nest? Or carry it off into a genuine forest? The stones of the wall were seeping and green. For the present she'd stay where she was.

The memory returned of the meat, of the woman whose bones she had scraped, of the dead cells of the woman in her own body, of their progress: stomach, mucous membranes, dispersion through her blood, black faeces already forming in her intestines, in addition to what they had already deposited on the trackside, she and the dog. In these two bodies, complicit in infamy, demons were feeding blazing furnaces with giant shovels. It was a fire of which she had previously had no inkling. She slept impatiently, the dog lying up against her stomach.

*Song of the Huntress:*
*Man or beast dead and best of all alive I am your fate I am your fate I snatch you from the earth and give you back to it your heart full or empty I eat and your soul*
*I drink it*
*I annihilate it.*

Bibliography and Acknowledgements

# BIBLIOGRAPHY

'Child of Evil Stars' ('L'Infortunée'): first French publication in *Lamont* (Le Visage vert, 2009). First English publication in *Postscript* no 24-25, April 2011 (PS Publishing).

'Fox into Lady' ('Fox into Lady'): first French publications in *Le Zaporogue* no 6 (June 2009) and *The Quarterly* no1 (Zanzibar, mars 2010).

'The Old Towpath': first publication in *Black Herald Magazine* no 1 (January 2011).

'The Opening' ('La Brèche'): first French publication in *Le Zaporogue* no 8 (June 2010).

'Meannanaich' ('Meannanaich'): first French publication in *Le Visage vert* no 9 (October 2000). First English publication in *Strange Tales* (Tartarus Press, 2003).

'Passing Forms' ('Le Cortège'): first French publication in *Lamont* (Le Visage vert, 2009).

'Under the Lighthouse' ('Au pied du phare'): first French publication in *Le Zaporogue* no 10 (June 2011).

'Pan's Children' ('Sur la Thay'): first French publication in *Lamont* (Le Visage vert, 2009).

'The Invention of Brunel' ('L'invention de Brunel'): first French publication in *Lamont* (Le Visage vert, 2009).

'Shioge' ('La Fin de la nuit'): first French publication in *Le Visage vert* no 12 (October 2002).

'What the Eye Remembers' ('Mémoire de l'œil'): first English publication in *Strange Tales, volume II* (Tartarus Press, 2007); first French publication in *Le Visage vert* no 15 (June 2008).

'Hilda' ('Hilda'): first French publication in *Lamont* (Le Visage vert, 2009).

'Lamont' ('Lamont'): first French publication in *Lamont* (Le Visage vert, 2009).

'Feral' ('Vivre sauvage dans les villes'): no previous publication.

# ACKNOWLEDGEMENTS

Many of these stories would not have written but for the wry and inalterable support of my friends Xavier Legrand-Ferronnière, Anne Guesdon, Blandine Longre, Paul Stubbs, Florence Prévost and Stepan Ueding. To Sébastien Doubinsky I owe the thrill of being considered a 'genuine Gothic lady'. And to Willie Charlton a nimble translation into English of all these tales and pieces, except for 'The Old Towpath', which was written directly into some sort of Saxonic language. *Darkscapes* would not, of course, exist without Rosalie Parker and Ray Russell, gatekeepers of Tartarus and much, much more.

Also available from Tartarus Press

# Limited edition hardback books from Tartarus Press

Aickman, Robert
*We Are for the Dark* (with
    Elizabeth Jane Howard)
*Dark Entries*
*Powers of Darkness*
*Sub Rosa*
*Cold Hand in Mine*
*Tales of Love and Death*
*Intrusions*
*Night Voices*
*The Attempted Rescue*
*The River Runs Uphill*

Barker, Nugent
*Written With My Left Hand*

Caveliero, Glen
*The Justice of the Night*

Collier, John
*Green Thoughts and Other
    Stories*

Crawford, F. Marion
*Uncanny Tales*

David, Charles
*The Way Things End*

Eisele, Michael
*The Girl with the Peacock Harp*
*Tree Spirit and Other Strange
    Tales*

Gaskin, John
*The New Inn Hall Deception*

Gautier, Theophile
*Clarimonde and Other Stories*

Hartley, L.P.
*The Collected Macabre Stories*

Harvey, W.F.
*The Double Eye*

Heuler, Karen
*The Clockworm and Other
    Strange Tales*

Hoffmann, E.T.A.
*The Sand-Man and Other Night
    Pieces*

Holmes, Carly
*Figurehead*

Howard, John, and Valentine,
    Mark
*Inner Europe*

Hughes, Rhys
*Orpheus on the Underground*

Lorrain, Jean
*Monsieur de Phocas*

Lloyd, Rebecca
*The Child Cephalina*
*Seven Strange Stories*
*Mercy and Other Stories*

Machen, Arthur
*Hieroglyphics*
*The London Adventure*
*The Autobiography of Arthur
Machen*
*The Children of the Pool*
*The Cosy Room*

McQueen, Magda
*Mirror Dead*

Murray, Walter J.C.
*Copsford*

Parker, Rosalie
*Strange Tales Volume II*
*Strange Tales Volume III*
*Strange Tales Volume IV*
*Strange Tales Volume V*

Poe, Edgar Alan
*The Macabre Tales*

Reynier, Michael
*Horthólary: Tales from
Montagascony*

Russell, R.B.
*Occult Territory: An Arthur
Machen Gazetteer*

Saint-Cyr, Jacques-Antoine
Révéroni, baron de
*Pauliska, or, Modern Perversity*

Sarban
*Ringstones*
*The Sound of His Horn and
Other Stories*

Stevenson, Robert Louis
*The Suicide Club and Other
Dark Adventures*

Strong, L.A.G.
*The Buckross Ring*

Symons, A.J.A.
*The Quest for Corvo*

Valentine, Mark
*A Wild Tumultory Library*
*Time, A Falconer: A Study of
Sarban*
with John Howard
*Inner Europe*

Van Rijswijk, Philomena
*House of the Flight-helpers*

Watt, D.P.
*Petals and Violins*

Wyckoff, Jason A.
*The Hidden Back Room*

# Paperbacks from Tartarus Press

Alain-Fournier
*Le Grand Meaulnes* and *Miracles*

Carlson, Eric Stener
*The St Perpetuus Club of Buenos Aires*
*Muladona*

Crisp, Quentin S.
*Morbid Tales*

Dobson, Roger
*Library of the Lost*

Gaskin, John
*The Long Retreating Day*
*The Master of the House*

Gawsworth, John
*The Life of Arthur Machen*

Howard, John, and Mark Valentine
*Secret Europe*
*The Collected Connoisseur*

Hughes, Rhys
*Worming the Harpy*

Lane, Joel
*This Spectacular Darkness*

Machen, Arthur
*Dreads and Drolls*
*The 1890s Notebook*
*The House of the Hidden Light*

Oliver, Reggie
*Holidays from Hell*
*Masques of Satan*
*The Dreams of Cardinal Vittorini*

*The Complete Symphonies of Adolf Hitler*
*Flowers of the Sea*
*Mrs Midnight and Other Stories*
*The Ballet of Dr Caligari*

Parker, Rosalie
*The Old Knowledge*

Parker Russell, Timothy, ed
*Dark World*

Russell, R.B.
*Putting the Pieces in Place* and *Literary Remains*
*Leave Your Sleep*

Anne-Sylvie Salzman
*Dearkscapes*

Samuels, Mark
*The White Hands*

Shiel, M.P.
*The Purple Cloud*

Slatter, Angela
*Sourdough and Other Stories*
*The Bitterwood Bible and Other Recountings*

Sulway, Nike
*Rupetta*

Valentine, Mark
*A Country Still All Mystery*
*Haunted by Books*
*Herald of the Hidden*
with John Howard
*Secret Europe*
*The Collected Connoisseur*

Printed in Great Britain
by Amazon

65770242R00123